It's America, 1940. Hostilities have kicked off in Europe, but Congress has passed the Neutrality Act, making it illegal for any American citizen to get involved in any way. It's in this atmosphere that Matthew Cooper, a civilian pilot for many years, decides to take up his friend, Debbie Douglas' offer of assistance to get overseas.

Tallyho
Copyright © 2024 Jon Bradbury
ISBN: 978-1-4874-4222-4
Cover art by Martine Jardin

Published by eXtasy Books Inc

Look for us online at:
www.eXtasybooks.com

Tallyho

By

Jon Bradbury

DEDICATION

An estimated three thousand pilots flew for the Royal Air Force during the four months of the Battle of Britain. They are known as The Few.

Prologue: The Diary

My wife Annie and I were just sitting down to dinner when the phone rang. I'd been home for about an hour, having flown tourists in a helicopter from the airport to the docks. Now we were getting ready to sit down for dinner.

Annie frowned. "Who could that be?"

"Probably one of those stupid telemarketers," I said.

She stepped over to the phone and lifted it. "Hello. Oh, hi, Mom."

I smiled. I still remember what my mom had told Annie, nervous at meeting my parents for the very first time. "*Call me Mom.*"

But just a moment later, Annie handed me the phone. "She says she needs to speak with you."

"Okay." I took the phone from her. "Hi, Mom."

There was a long silence on the line, punctuated only by a *sniff*.

"Mom?" I said, less sure of myself.

There was another sniff. "He's gone, Matt. Your granddad, Matt, the first."

I was left gobsmacked, blindsided, a bite of whatever it was I was about to eat, halfway to my mouth, forgotten. "What?"

"I know you two were close," she said. "That's where you got your love of flying and airplanes from."

I chuckled sadly. I still had that model *Spitfire*. Granddad had taught me how to fly an airplane before I could even drive a car. Before I got my learner's permit, I already had my pilot's license. At school, I had a special kind of confidence.

1

When I graduated high school, I went to learn how to fly private jets, after which I got a job ferrying celebrities here and there. Just for the fun of it, I'd learned how to fly helicopters so I could start ferrying tourists from the airport. I have a comfortable lifestyle and travel often.

I asked her, "Uhm . . . did they say how he died?"

Annie gasped and covered her mouth. I dropped my fork, took her hand in my own free hand, and squeezed it.

Meanwhile, mom said, "The nursing home said he had a heart attack and died in his sleep. At least he went peacefully. Frankly, I'm surprised he's lasted this long. The man was in his nineties."

I heard another sniff. Trying to comfort her, I said, "Well, now he's with Grandma."

Grandma, Catherine Cooper, had passed away the year before. I'd seen pictures of her when she was young, both of when she'd been working for *Pan Am* and during her war service with the US Eighth Air Force in England doing what she had already been doing, just with a different uniform on. She was, simply put, beautiful, as women from that period tended to be.

I personally would've given anything for one more *dear* from her.

Then Mom continued, sounding stronger and more in control of herself. "Sometime next week, the family is going to get together for the reading of the will. Try to be there. I know he left you something. I just don't know what."

"Uhm, yeah. I'll be there." I spoke in a dull, mechanical voice.

"He's living forever in the clouds," Mom said. "Just where he wanted to be."

That finally brought a smile to my face. "Yeah," I said. "You guys need anything? Anything I can get for you, anything I can bring you?"

"No, son. We'll be fine. At least I think we will be. If I need anything, you'll be the next to know."

"Okay, Mom."

"Bye, son."

"Bye, Mom. Love you, guys."

"Love you, too, son. Bye-bye."

"Bye, Mom." And we hung up.

Just as promised, there was a reading of the will a few days later. Granddad Matt had left me a monetary gift, which he'd given to everyone in the family. But he'd gifted me something that he hadn't given anyone else in the family, something even my sister Emily wasn't jealous of, something unexpected — a letter with mysterious instructions.

I said to Granddad's estate attorney, "What's this?"

"Sorry, that's what he specified in his will."

"Yeah, I see that," I said. I turned to Annie and said, "Feel like a trip overseas?"

"I'd love to."

"Great," I said, reading the additional instructions. "It says here we have forty-eight hours to pack for our flight."

"Excellent," she said. "I've always wanted to see London!"

Two days later, Annie and I were arriving at LaGuardia. Apparently, instructions had been sent before us, and as our taxi pulled up to the terminal, there was a lady waiting for us, dressed in a very prim and proper suit, her auburn hair only a shade or two lighter than Annie's, was pinned up in an equally proper bun.

"Mister Cooper?" she asked, extending her hand.

"Yes," I said, taking her hand.

"Jane Thomas. I represent an organization that seeks to preserve any artifacts relating to the Second World War and any related events. Yes?"

I said, "Uhm, I gotta tell you now. Don't be surprised if I have no idea what you're talking about. Granddad never talked about what he did in the war."

She gave a single nod in understanding. "Quite so. Not many of them do. So I will do my best to, how do you Americans say, cushion the blow. But I must tell you now, in return, that you are in for quite a few surprises."

"Like what?" I asked, feeling a frown on my face.

"Well, I don't know if you're familiar with the Eagle Squadrons?"

I said, "That's a group of American pilots that flew for the Royal Air Force before the United States entered the war."

"That's correct," she said. "Well, your grandfather was one of them."

I reeled. It was like an emotional gut punch. I literally had to stop and sit down on a nearby bench. All these years and granddad never said a thing — to me or to anyone in the family.

"Are you all right?" Jane asked, sounding concerned for the first time.

"Yeah," I said. "I'm all right. Or will be. I need a drink."

A tiny smile came and went on Jane's face. "Yes, I quite understand. It's a lot to take in. This way, shall we? We have a private jet waiting."

After a Transatlantic flight, Annie and I found ourselves in jolly old London, England. Annie found much to occupy her interest while I took a taxi to the RAF Museum in central London.

There, an elderly gentleman greeted me with a piercing stare and a nod before I could even introduce myself. His hair had long since turned white, but his eyes were dark blue and keen. "I know who you are. I can see the resemblance. You're Matt Cooper's grandson, am I right?"

Stunned, I only said, "Yes! How did you—"

He gave another nod. "Yes. I rather thought so. It's not hard to tell. You look quite a lot like him."

"You knew him?"

"Yes, indeed, I did," he said. "Flew with him, in fact."

"I'm sorry," I said. "I don't even know who you are . . ."

He suddenly cracked a grin. "Sorry, getting ahead of myself. Vern Holliday."

I extended my hand. "Matt Cooper," I said. "But I guess you knew that."

"Come over here. We have something for you." That *something* turned out to be a large box.

I asked, "Do you know what's in here?"

Holliday smiled an enigmatic smile. "I'm afraid I don't know, not exactly," he told me. "Only one way to find out."

"Right," I replied. "So let's do it."

"That's the spirit, lad." Holliday flicked open a switchblade knife with a deadpan aplomb and helped me break the seal on the box, which was heavily, securely taped.

The first thing I found in the box were side panels from three airplanes—the first one being from a *P-51 Mustang*, the second from a *P-47 Thunderbolt*, and the last one from a *Spitfire*, a plane that was legendary. Painted just under where the windscreen would have been was a name—Matthew Cooper. Below that was a row of swastikas.

Next to me, Holliday chuckled. "Kill markings," he said. "Your grandfather was a certified Ace."

"Are you serious?"

"Perfectly," he said. "Keep looking."

Under the panels were uniform sleeves, which I thought was odd until I realized that each sleeve was sky blue and had a stripe at the cuff. Each of the stripes was a lighter shade of blue and bordered in black. The first sleeve had a half-stripe, but there soon followed more sleeves, all the way up to a sleeve with two full stripes and a half-stripe in between.

Shit. Granddad was a Squadron Leader!

After that, however, was shoulder and collar insignia, shiny silver captain's bars against the dull, split-pea soup shade of green Army people wore, followed by bronze oak leaves indicating the rank of Major, followed in turn by silver oak leaves indicating he'd been a Lieutenant Colonel.

Along with the RAF sleeves, there was a piece of fabric in the same color with RAF pilot's wings. I closed my eyes for a moment. It was overwhelming.

After a moment, I resumed exploring, finding a flat box. "What's this?" I asked.

"Your grandfather's Distinguished Flying Cross," Holliday said.

"I'm sorry — his *what?*" I asked.

"Just keep going," Holliday said gently.

So I kept digging in the box, and I soon discovered some old photographs way down in the bottom, among which was a photograph of several men standing in front of a *Spitfire* fighter aircraft. I recognized my grandfather's face among all the others. The photographer had clearly captured a moment of humor. They were all laughing at something.

They were all young, carefree, and ready to give their lives for another country. I was stunned to see my face looking at me — tawny wheat-colored hair, hazel eyes, kind of a Paul Newman-esque face with a high forehead.

Way down at the bottom of the box was an old leather-bound diary, firmly secured with several rubber bands. "Look at this," I said to Holliday.

"Bloody hell," he said quietly.

"You never knew he wrote a diary?"

"I thought he'd been writing letters to home," he said.

I gently took off the rubber bands and gingerly opened the cover. As I did so, three things fell out on the floor — two sets of dog tags that jingled when they fell out, which I put in my pocket, and a folded piece of note paper.

I quickly picked it up, but I very carefully unfolded it. It was dated July of 1969 — the week of my birthday! Preparing myself for more potentially shocking revelations, I read the note.

Matthew the third,

As I write this, you haven't even been born yet. My son, your father, Matthew the second, keeps telling my daughter-in-law, your mother, to have the baby for his birthday. We keep trying to tell him that such things can't be scheduled. You're their first baby so, more than likely, you're going to be late. I personally hope you won't be born on the day they launch the moon mission.

Just last week I spoke to my estate attorney about bequeathing you all of my war things in my will. I've never told anyone about what happened to me before America entered the war, but I feel as if it's important for you to know what I did and why I did it.

I've carried this diary around since the end of the war, and no-body has read it — not even your grandmother, Catherine. It covers the time from when war broke out in September of 1939, all the way up to when the United States declared war on Japan in December of 1941, and for a few months after. You'll soon see why.

I hope you treasure this diary.

Your grandfather,

Matthew Cooper

That was the end of the note. I flipped the paper over, hoping to see more, but there was nothing more to read. I looked up to see the old man gazing at me with a kindly expression. "I know, it's a lot to take in."

"You could say that," I replied, sounding like I felt — like I'd been hit with a ton of bricks and punched in the gut, emotionally speaking.

"Would you like some assistance getting this box to your hotel?"

"Yes, please," I said. "That would be very kind of you."

"Not at all," he said, gruffly but kindly. "Let's get this box squared away."

Once I got back to our hotel, I returned to the diary and opened it again. The first entry was, as the letter said, dated September 1, 1939—the date of the German invasion of Poland in Europe.

As I started to read, the room fell away . . .

CHAPTER ONE

Friday, 1 September 1939

I *went to the news stand down the street from my apartment build-ing to buy a newspaper as soon as I'd heard the news on the radio, once I'd been home from work. The New York Times had the headline* HITLER INVADES POLAND *prominently plastered across its front page.*

War had officially broken out in Europe. I say officially because the latest move by Nazi Germany, to invade Poland, had, according to the article, resulted in an unprecedented move by Great Britain and France to send their ambassadors to their respective German embassies to request an immediate cessation of hostilities – or a state of war would be in effect.

We were still waiting for word back on what the German ambas-sador has to say to the British and French. More than likely there's going to be an official state of war before too long.

I don't know if anyone is going to read this diary after all is said and done, but I will do my best to keep you updated on all that hap-pens.

The sky was as clear as you could ask for. I could literally see forever.

The sun was shining. There wasn't a cloud in the sky to spoil this otherwise idyllic late summer day in New York City. I was flying about a thousand feet above it all, literally speaking. I was at the controls of a silver *DC-2*.

I reached down for the radio transmitter. "*Pan Am* Nancy Carol one-five-zero-zero-seven requesting permission to land, over."

"LaGuardia to *Pan Am*. Follow your current heading out over the water for one-zero miles, then come right to two-six-five degrees for final approach. Over."

"Roger, LaGuardia. Will do."

"Welcome to LaGuardia."

Ten minutes later, the runways of LaGuardia Airport were coming into view. I reached up and flipped the switches to extend the landing gear, while my co-pilot set the flaps correctly.

Another five minutes and we'd come to a stop at the end of the runway. Pulling the engine throttles all the way down to idle, we taxied off the runway and over to our gate. Even as we finally turned the engines off, I looked back and saw a boarding ladder was already being wheeled into place at the rear of the aircraft, allowing our passengers to deplane. We were finally home.

I took off the radio headset, unstrapped the aircraft, and lastly made a notation in the logbook. Then both of us stood up and headed for the hatch directly behind us.

Carrying our suitcases, we headed for the *Pan Am* office.

The relative quiet of the employee's lounge wasn't the usual sort of quiet. That made me a little uneasy. My copilot and I, Christopher Edwards, both made our way over to the check-in desk to sign the logbook to let the boss know we were alive.

The clerk, Julia Hawthorne, had us sign in like usual. She was young, blonde, and pretty. At the moment, she was wearing a white silk blouse tucked into a navy-blue suspender skirt, her blonde hair in a proper bun, legs in sheer nude seamed stockings, and heels on her feet. Except she, too, wasn't quite her usual self.

So finally I asked, "What on earth's happened? It feels like there's been a funeral or something."

Julia gave me a look. "Close enough."

"What do you mean?"

"Listen to this." She turned around, walked over to the radio in the far corner, and turned up the volume. A commercial was just ending.

A male voice came on. *"This is Jack Homer with ABC Radio Network. If you're just joining us, let's catch you up on current events. At midnight local time, according to the Associated Press bureau chief in Warsaw, the Germany Army and Air Force have crossed over the border in force—"*

Chris and I both squawked, "What?"

Julia shushed us.

"The Germans have already captured several small villages along the border into Poland, and are, according to reports, running roughshod over Polish air and ground forces, using cooperative tactics best described as lightning war or Blitzkrieg. The British and the French have each sent a diplomat to their respective German embassies asking them to cease their operations at once or a state of war will exist between the three nations."

I looked at Chris and said, "Holy shit. War."

"Yeah, sounds like this is it."

Julia, sounding worried, asked, "Do you think we'll be in it soon?"

Chris confidently said, "Nah, it's all the way over there. Come on."

Privately, I wasn't quite so sure. But I said, "Thanks, Julia."

"Sure, sweetie. You guys take care."

We both proceeded past the front desk and into the back room. Even Chris was quiet as we headed past the back rooms and out the door, back into daylight, and headed to the subway station a block away from the airport.

As we walked outside, I observed, "You're awfully quiet, Chris."

He said, "This is big, Matt."

I didn't have to ask him what *this* was. I just let him continue. And he did.

"I mean, maybe Hitler's finally gone too far. The British have never sent someone to the German embassy like that before, not even when they invaded Czechoslovakia."

With a cringe, I remembered that day earlier in the year.

Over the last several years, the British Prime Minister, Neville Chamberlain, had been practicing a policy known as appeasement with regard to Hitler and his plans for Europe in the interests of maintaining peace, which basically meant letting Hitler have his way with no consequences. But now it appeared as though Hitler had finally gone too far.

After a moment's silence, I said, "Well, for the moment anyway, we don't even know what this is, although I agree it's looking bad. Come on, let's stop by the watering hole and get a beer. I could use a drink, and I know you could, too."

"Yeah," he said. "If we get to the station in time, we can make the subway and be home before dinner."

At that time, my family was glad that I'd taken a lucrative though routine job as a pilot with *Pan Am*. Just three years ago, in 1936, I'd graduated from high school, walked right out of graduation, and headed to the nearest Army Recruiting Center to apply with the Army Air Corps as a flight cadet, where I'd washed out, found to be *lacking in intrinsic flying ability*, as the letter had put it.

I took that letter and the officer who'd written it, Major Nathan *Nate* Hughes, with a grain of salt. For some US Army Air Corps staff-puke to tell me I couldn't fly an airplane was adding insult to injury.

My mother had been profoundly relieved when I'd washed out, but I'd been profoundly crushed. My dad was a little more understanding, but he'd also counseled me to take my flying experience and perhaps use it in a different way.

I'd been flying airplanes and fixing airplane engines since before I could even drive a car, starting with the family crop-duster on the farm in upstate New York. It was a two-seater *Fokker* biplane, older than I was, painted bright yellow, and given somewhat of an upgrade after Dad and my uncle had refitted her with a more powerful engine — an air-cooled radial engine. I had longed to fly her, and a few weeks later, I got my wish.

My uncle had been teaching me how to fly the year I started high school, but I hadn't taken a solo flight until one day, my dad had fallen ill with the flu and could barely even get out of bed, while my uncle was away on business. So at the age of fifteen, I got his blessing to fly the family crop duster.

My mom wasn't quite so sure. She wanted me to keep my feet firmly planted on the ground, but naturally, Dad, being a man, wanted me to fly the family crop duster. So on that clear morning in May of 1934, I took to the air solo, and I found it was the most natural thing I'd ever done. It felt as though me and the airplane were melded together somehow.

In high school, I had a confidence I couldn't hide. The first time you fly an airplane without someone in the back seat, it tends to boost your confidence. I graduated to the mail plane a year later when the regular pilot had come down with pneumonia and couldn't go to the bathroom without coughing, let alone fly an airplane.

Granted, the mail plane getting through wasn't a matter of life or death, but for the people of the small town I'd flown to with their mail, it was important enough that I got a chance to fly something else besides the family crop duster that day, a twin-engine floatplane with twin rudders and a big glassed-in cockpit.

But something else just as important happened that day. I landed the plane in the lake, tied up alongside the dock, and climbed out — to see a petite, curvy brunette beauty with silky black hair, pale skin, and blue eyes, wearing a bustier top and denim cut-offs with bare feet. She was round, firm, and she was fully packed. Then she smiled at me.

"Uhm, hi," I said, heart racing all of a sudden.

"Hi," she said with a southern accent. "Please tell me you have the mail in that airplane. My Aunt Grace is going to absolutely have a heart attack if the mail isn't here."

I cracked a grin despite the seriousness of the moment. "Yep. Got it right here. I don't suppose you all have a mail carrier around here?"

The smile widened. "I think I can get him." I found out later her name was Cathy, and I had her phone number in the pocket of my flight jacket before I left for New York.

With the mailman's help, we got the mail unloaded. The council was so grateful they hired me on the spot to be a relief pilot. I was sixteen years old. I flew for them for two more years, until I graduated from high school and applied to the US Army Air Corps. Every time I flew out to that tiny village by the lake, Cathy and I . . . caught up. I would've called on the telephone as often as I could, but long-distance calls were expensive.

After I washed out, I picked up my broken heart and applied at *Pan Am* the next day. Their standards were much easier to satisfy — all it took was to have a pilot's license — and I soon found myself a pilot for *Pan Am*, flying a route between LaGuardia and Chicago. It took about a year for me to be promoted from First Officer to Captain, which my parents were quick to point out to all their friends. They were so proud of me. But I had bigger dreams than that, bigger fish to fry.

As my grandmother was fond of saying, the Lord works in mysterious ways. Maybe I was just being saved for something else. If I couldn't fly for Uncle Sam, maybe I could fly for someone else.

While the civilian airline industry was flying some of the finest flying machines in the air, the US military and the Navy were flying biplanes that weren't much different from planes flown in the First World War — *biplanes*, I tell you.

Overseas was a different story. Germany had started coming out with the most advanced flying machines ever built, machines built with all metal construction and other advanced features. Willy Messerschmitt had debuted his *BF-109* fighter plane at an air show in 1936, and it had left everything else in the dust. It was faster than anything that flew at the air show, and it was a grim omen of things to come. Naturally, the British had started its own aircraft-building program, years behind the Germans, but they were rapidly catching up.

At the moment, the holiday weekend beckoned. War or not, there was a three-day weekend ahead, and I intended to take advantage of it, and so did Chris.

A barbecue was calling, a day spent with friends, celebrating the end of summer.

CHAPTER TWO

Friday, 1 March, 1940

A ll is quiet on the western front — for the time being. It took the *Germans a month to conquer Poland. It goes without saying there's an official state of war in effect between Great Britain, France, and Nazi Germany.*

Since then, all has been quiet, although there have been rumblings of war in Finland and Norway, and British ships have been sunk by German submarines in the North Atlantic. One senator was quoted in the papers as saying, "There's something phoney about this war." *So naturally, the papers have started calling it the Phoney War, even as they're covering all this stuff.*

I bumped into Debbie Douglas the other day, a friend of mine. She says she knows people who can get me in with the RAF in England—if I'm still eager to join the war, which I am. She says she works for an organization called The Clayton Knight Committee. I have no idea who that even is.

But she wouldn't say anything more than that, and I know why. Thanks to the Neutrality Act, it's a federal felony to even think about fighting for a nation involved in the hostilities, even if it's an allied nation.

I'm meeting her next week at the Waldorf Astoria in Manhattan. Just don't tell anyone, especially Mom and Dad. They would kill me.

While I had some time off, one day bright and early, I got dressed in my best suit and tie and took the subway to Manhattan. I got off at the right stop, climbed the stairs to street level, and walked about a block over to Park Avenue, where the Waldorf Astoria Hotel was. It was a quite famous hotel, made that way by a list of celebrities who called the hotel *home* every now and then.

As I walked along, my copilot and erstwhile buddy, Christopher Edwards, walked along with me, not bothering to lower his voice, but also glancing suspiciously at everyone and everything.

"Man, are you sure you want to do this?" he asked me.

I rounded on him. "Listen, I'm not *doing* anything, not at the moment, except meeting a friend of mine. So would you shut up, already? Do you want us to get arrested?"

"Okay. I'm sorry. I still can't believe I joined you when you signed up for a transfer to London."

"Yeah, well, nobody made you do that," I reminded him, resuming my stroll. "And as for transferring to England, right now, it's quieter than a church over there. So why not?"

I reached the street corner across from Park Avenue and had to stop while I waited for the light to turn green. Once I crossed the street, I was promptly greeted by Debbie Douglas herself, looking quite lovely, dressed against the March chill in a dark navy-blue dress, dark-colored trench coat, and high heels. Her auburn hair was done up in curls, and she was wearing makeup, making her look like Lana Turner.

"There you are," she said, all smiles as she stepped up and gave me a quick kiss on the cheek.

"Hi," I said. "You look spiffy."

"Why, this old thing?" she asked with a cocked eyebrow. "But thank you. I see you brought a friend —"

"It's okay," I told her, heading her off. "He's a co-worker."

She gazed long and hard at him for a few moments, then at me. "You might regret that," she said quietly. "We might all regret that. But come on. This way."

I didn't get the chance to ask her what I might have regretted because she turned on the spot and led us into the hotel lobby. Once inside, she punched the call button for the elevator, which arrived only a few moments later, and we stepped on. She quickly punched the button for the tenth floor. Only a few moments later, the elevator opened onto a quiet hallway, where she stepped off again at once, turned left, and started walking down the hallway.

She stopped at a set of double doors. Over the doorway was a plain sign that simply said *The Clayton Knight Committee.*

"This way, gentlemen," she said, holding the door open for us.

Without a word, I stepped through the door —

Into a fully functioning office.

Just inside the doorway, a lady sat at a desk to the right of the door. Beyond that, another lady sat, taking someone's information. Beyond that, yet another lady, this one wearing a white nurse's uniform, was taking a man's blood pressure.

The lady at the first desk looked up at us and smiled. "Welcome to the Clayton Knight Committee. Oh, hi, Debbie. New recruits?"

Debbie glanced back at us as she took off her trench coat and hung it up, then at her colleague. "Yes, Veronica. I hope so."

Veronica, the woman at the desk, said, "You gentlemen want to fly for the Royal Air Force?"

We both said, "Yes, ma'am."

Veronica smiled ever so slightly. "Right this way. Let's get you started." She rose from her desk and led me to another lady seated behind the second desk, who looked up as we approached.

"What do we have here, Veronica?"

"Annie, can you get these men processed, please?"

Annie, a rather attractive blonde, smiled at me as she fed a new form into her typewriter, turning the knob with confidence. "Sure. You first. Have a seat, sweetheart."

I did so rather hesitantly, but I sat down all the same. I was wondering what I was getting myself into, reminding myself this *was* what I wanted.

"Your full name, sweetheart. Last name first." She waited, fingers daintily poised on the keys of her typewriter.

So I gave her my info, and she typed away.

Cooper, Matthew Joseph.

Age. Social security number. Place and date of birth. Occupation.

Her eyes widened slightly as I told her my job as an airline pilot.

Then there were still more questions. Medical questions. Finally, after about half an hour, she said, "Sit tight, Matthew. I'm going to go see if the nurse is free so she can take your vitals."

"Okay . . ."

Annie rose at once from her desk and went over to the nurse. They talked for a moment or two, then Annie returned. "Okay, Matthew. Marie here can take you."

Marie, the nurse, was a brunette, with fine features and a nice smile, dressed in a spanking white uniform, including cap, sneakers, and red lipstick. "Come on over here so I can take your vitals." There followed a series of quick, matter-of-fact, no-nonsense checks—blood pressure, pulse, vision, and temperature, which she entered on the form.

Once all that was done, she said, "Wait right here while I check if the doctor is available to start your physical exam."

"Right."

More than an hour later, after an exhaustive physical exam, I was in an office with an older gentleman, who had the look of someone who'd been around the block. Once the doctor had finished with me, I was shown into an office where this man held court, holding the folder containing my file.

"I see you've been a pilot for a few years now," he said, looking up from it.

"Yes, sir," I said. "Since high school."

"Indeed. So tell me, old boy, why do you want to fly for the Royal Air Force? I don't have to tell you that you'd be risking rather a lot."

I swallowed. I knew what he meant—I would be risking more than just my life by flying for the Royal Air Force. If arrested by the FBI, tried, and found guilty of breaking the Neutrality Act, I could have faced jail time—and worse. I could have lost my *citizenship*.

More than likely, my family would have disowned me. They were fervently isolationist.

I said, "It's just a matter of time before America is involved in the war. Besides that, I'm a good pilot, and while we aren't involved just yet, I can still fly for someone else."

"Well, you've passed your physical exam brilliantly, so you're cleared to fly," he said.

"Thanks," I said.

The man smiled ever so slightly. Then he said, "I understand you fly for *Pan Am*."

That was an odd question. Thrown by the sudden change in subject, I answered him all the same, "Yes. That's right."

"Good. Your contact at the airline is a man named James Madison. He will go over the next steps."

I blinked in surprise. *Jimmie?* Quiet, unassuming Jimmie, who I'd spoken with over the last few weeks about transferring overseas? What did he have to do with all this?

"Uhm, what do you mean, next steps?"

His smile widened just noticeably. "Jimmie is going to assist you with your journey to England so it won't look quite so suspicious to the Feds."

I rose from my chair, extending my hand. "I see. Thanks

for your time today."

"Not at all, old boy." He took my hand in a warm, firm grip. "Violet will see you out. In the meantime, take this with you." He placed the file folder in my free hand. "You'll need this in London. They'll aid in your processing with the Royal Air Force training chaps, you see. That way, you won't have to go through the physical all over again."

"Right," I said. "Thanks again."

"Not at all," he said. "And do take care over there, old boy."

From the hotel, Chris and I went straight over to LaGuardia. We even took a cab, not wanting to wait for the next subway across town. Once we arrived, we first went into the *Pan Am* offices, where Julia looked up at our entrance and said, "Oh, good, you're here. Mr. Madison wants to see you."

Chris and I exchanged glances. Then I told her, "We'll go see him. Thanks, Julia."

She smiled. "Sure, sweetie."

As soon as we made our appearance at the receptionist's desk in front of Jimmie's office, the girl spoke before I could even so much as say *hello*. "Captain Cooper, there you are."

"Hi, Mary Jane," I said. "What's—"

"Mr. Madison wants to see you about your transfer request."

That took the wind out of my sails, so to speak, but only for a minute. After all, I wanted to see him, too. "Uhm, yeah. Of course."

"Have a seat," she said. "Let me just make sure he's not on a phone call."

"Right. I'll just wait here." So Chris and I sat and waited like good boys.

Next to me, Chris grunted his disbelief. "What's this world coming to?"

"Having a hard time wrapping your head around it?" I asked him.

"And you're not?" he asked.

"Of course I am," I said. "I never suspected a thing."

Chris grunted again but didn't reply.

I couldn't believe that Jimmy was a double agent for the Clayton Knight Committee. Granted, the Committee was recruiting for the Royal Air Force, but it was the principle of the thing. At the same time, this simplified things.

My folks hadn't been happy at all when I brought up the subject of transferring overseas over dinner at home a few days ago. Dad nearly spit out his beer. Mom had *disapproval* written all over her face. I told a little white lie and said the company was making me transfer, that it wasn't my idea. That seemed to satisfy them. I sure as hell wasn't about to tell them the truth—that not only was it my idea, but that I'd requested a transfer to England.

The mood in the nation, twenty years after the end of the First World War, was still firmly anti-war, or more specifically, strictly isolationist. In the aftermath of the Armistice that officially ended the war, the United States completely pulled back from world affairs. The entire world could have been going up in flames, and we wouldn't have cared so long as it didn't involve any Americans. But there were some, like myself, who believed it was just a matter of time until the US got involved. Although, one couldn't blame the casual observer for thinking the war was going nowhere.

By the winter of 1940, a curious calm had settled down over the Continent, an uneasy state of waiting that felt like the calm before the storm. One US Senator had called it the *Phoney War*, some papers calling the war *Sitzkrieg*, and the name had stuck, a play on the term *Lightning War* or *Blitzkrieg*. The worst part was that nobody had any idea of if or when the storm might have broken, which was why my mom and dad weren't terribly thrilled about me getting transferred overseas to London.

At that moment, Jimmie's secretary came out and said, "Captain Cooper? Mr. Madison will see you now." And she held the door open for me.

I rose from my chair, aware that this would pretty much seal my fate. "What about Chris?"

"Mr. Madison said to send you in first," she told me.

"Okay. Thanks," I said, stepping across the threshold.

She closed the door behind me. Quiet settled down almost at once.

I said, "You wanted to see me, Jimmie?"

He looked up from his papers at my entrance. Jimmie Madison was not what I would have expected out of an airline executive—short and stocky like a pilot, possessed of a thick head-full of straight auburn hair and piercing green eyes.

"Have a seat, Cooper." I did so, and he continued. "Well, I won't beat about the bush. Your transfer has been approved."

"Great," I said. "I was told to show you these."

There was a twinkle in Jimmie's eyes as he took the documents from me and glanced at them. "Ah," he said, handing them back to me. "I didn't think there would have been any trouble."

"No. It took them a while, but they said I'm cleared to fly."

"Good. If you're ready to leave for London, there's a *Clipper* plane leaving at eleven this Thursday morning for Lisbon, Portugal. From there, you can catch a connecting flight to London."

Just enough time to get ready. "Don't I need a ticket?"

"As an employee, no, you don't need a ticket. However, this should satisfy the ticket desk." And he handed me a letter, written on company letterhead, with a copy of my transfer. "Keep that with your, uh, *other* paperwork."

I couldn't hold it in anymore. "For Christ's sake, Jimmy," I burst out. "The Clayton Knight Committee?"

He asked me bluntly, "What are you getting your panties in a twist over?"

"We can't afford to have you get yourself arrested," I told him.

"Thanks," he told me, smiling briefly. "But let me ask you, have any government agents been sniffing your tail today?"

I blinked. "No," I realized. "Not even when I went to meet Debbie Douglas . . ."

Jimmie winked. "Lovely girl, that Debbie," he said, returning to the documents on his desk. "It was her idea for me to get involved, actually."

I shook my head, mostly to myself. I couldn't believe there was an underground conspiracy to get Americans overseas to fight for someone else — and that President Roosevelt was having the FBI turn a blind eye to its activity.

Facing me, he suddenly said, "Listen, you have every right to be concerned. But this is going to help you get to London, right?"

"Right," I said.

"So please try to relax," he told me. "You'll be in London before you know it, flying for the Royal Air Force and wondering what all the fuss was about."

Keeping up the pretense, I said, "How long do you think I'll be in the London office?"

"I don't know," he answered honestly. "I expect you'll come home quickly enough if things go sideways in Europe. Oh, yeah, one more thing."

"Which is?"

"Until such time as you're accepted into the Royal Air Force flight training program, you're an employee of *Pan Am*. If an FBI agent were to question you in London, you've been given a corporate transfer and you're to give them the number for the London office if they have further questions."

"Got it," I said.

"Good," he said. "Any other questions?"

"Nope," I said. "I guess I'm all set, then."

"Yes," he said. "You're all set. Good luck in London. They're lucky to have you. You're one of our best pilots."

I wasn't sure who he was referring to. But all the same, I said, "Thanks."

Jimmie rose from behind his desk, extending his hand. "Take care over there, would you? I would hate to call your family to inform them of your passing."

"Right," I said dryly, taking his hand. "Guess I'd better get home and start packing."

"Yes, and you should get your affairs in order before you go overseas. Get out of here."

"Gone . . ."

"But first send in Christopher, would you?"

"Sure," I said.

Thursday morning, Chris and I took a taxi to La Guardia together.

On our way back home, Chris told me he'd gotten the same speech from Jimmie, including how to respond to any federal agents.

I found it altogether unsettling that we hadn't, in fact, been questioned or followed by any G-men, as Federal agents were known back then. Debbie had told me, like Jimmie had, that President Roosevelt had told the FBI to look the other way with regards to the Committee's activities. That explained a lot, in my mind. Still, I expected to see an FBI agent following me around, sticking his nose in my business.

But nobody had. Or maybe they were just being crafty about it.

To complete the fiction that we were just another couple of business travelers, we both decided to pack our uniforms but dress in civilian clothes, me in a shirt and tie, rumpled brown trousers, and a sweater vest with sneakers, while Chris went with a simple suit. We both carried our uniforms in a wardrobe case with our documents and shaving kits.

Once we got out of the cab at LaGuardia, we went across to the far side of the airport to the Marine Air Terminal. The plane wasn't scheduled to take off until eleven, so we both had plenty of time to get on board. Hopefully, the plane wasn't over-sold, or if it had been, hopefully, someone hadn't shown up.

That was my main thought as we went inside and approached the front ticket desk. The girl looked up at us with a friendly smile. "How can I help you gentlemen this morning?"

"My buddy and I are hoping to get on the *Clipper* flight to Lisbon. Can you squeeze us in?"

"Let me check first. Do you have a ticket?"

"No," I said.

"Then I'm afraid I can't—"

"But we have these." I handed her the letter Jimmie had given me, along with the approved transfer. Chris did the same.

She took our letters, read them from top to bottom, then handed them back. "I'm pretty sure we can squeeze you in, Captain Cooper, but let me check. I think so, but let me check."

"Okay," I said.

The girl left the desk and went through a door. She was gone quite a few minutes before she came back and said, "Yes. We can squeeze you in. Unfortunately, we have to put you in the front compartment, but we can squeeze you two in."

"That won't be a problem," I assured her.

Chris leaned in and said, "If they have to ditch at sea, we'll be the first to go."

I elbowed him in the ribs, urging him to hold his tongue. With an innocent look, he shut up.

"Do you gentlemen have any luggage with you?"

"Just carry-ons," I told her.

"Excellent," she replied. "If you two will follow me, I'll show you to the waiting area."

"After you," I said.

At the time of this story, in the winter of 1940, *Pan Am's Clipper* planes were some of the largest aircraft flying for civilian airlines, still in their gleaming natural metal finish, like the rest of their aircraft. They wouldn't get painted until the US entered the war.

They were built by *Boeing*, with four radial air-cooled, three-bladed propeller engines, and had the distinguishing feature of being a floatplane—a rarity at the time of our story. The designers also saw fit, for some reason, to give the plane both twin rudders and a single tail. No pilot would ever say no to that. It was also roomy, comfortable—and was only flown by experienced people with at least fifteen years in the company. It had a flight crew of five in the cockpit—pilot, co-pilot, radio operator, flight engineer, and navigator. Sorry, ladies—in 1940, the flight crew was all male.

I'm afraid I wouldn't have qualified because I've only been with the company less than five years, but somehow, I got this transfer to London. Go figure, huh?

I had a sneaking suspicion, confirmed by Jimmie, that *Pan Am* had a *quiet arrangement* with the Clayton Knight Committee, just as it had a quiet arrangement with President Roosevelt. I couldn't prove it, but at the same time, I also couldn't deny the ease with which I'd been processed and given a transfer to England—a transfer for which I had already applied, to be sure, but I was surprised to get, all the same.

Now Chris and I were sitting in the passenger lounge, waiting for our flight to be called, looking like just two more business travelers, although maybe not as well-dressed as some. We must have sat there for about half an hour when one of the flight attendants announced, "Ladies and gentlemen, we are now boarding. If you'll all follow me, please."

We all rose from our seats and followed her outside to a gorgeous sunny morning, with only a variety of white, high, thin clouds to spoil the view. We reached the walkway to the dock, where we had to follow her in single file. Fortunately, there was only about a dozen or so passengers, counting Chris and I.

Tied alongside the dock was the four-engine *Boeing* floatplane, with the name *Yankee Clipper* painted prominently on the fuselage just under the cockpit, along with a large American flag.

In no time, Chris and I were taking a seat in the forwardmost cabin. Surprisingly, we had the cabin to ourselves. Gratefully we tossed our luggage on one of the empty chairs and sat down to wait for takeoff.

Even better, we learned the stairway to the cockpit was in the compartment behind ours. I doubted that either of us would get called up to the cockpit, but it was nice to know.

As we took our seats and started getting ready for takeoff, a female voice with a genteel southern dialect came on and announced, "Ladies and gentlemen, this is Catherine, your flight stewardess. Please take your seats and get situated for taking off. We'll be slipping our moorings off in just a few minutes. Thank you for flying with us."

An hour later, the Atlantic Ocean was twenty-five thousand feet below us, a glittering plate of glass as far as the eye could see. The ride, I noticed, was just as smooth.

"Hi, boys—"

I looked up as a beautiful brunette wearing a blue *Pan Am* flight attendant's uniform came in, pushing along a little cart loaded with drinks, hair pinned back in a bun, just in time to see her face light up, as if in recognition. I'm sure there was a similar expression on my own face.

"Well, as I live and breathe," she said, sounding very southern. "Matthew Cooper!"

"Hi, Cathy," I said, rising from my seat to accept a hug.

"Hi," Chris said lamely.

Meanwhile, Cathy said, "I see the airline has been treating you rather nicely, Captain Cooper."

"Look at you," I said. "You haven't done so bad yourself. Working on a *Clipper* flight? How long have you worked for *Pan Am*?"

"About three years, now," she said. "There weren't many jobs in that small town, as you know. My aunt didn't live that long after you decided to apply to the Air Corps."

"Which I failed miserably at," I told her.

"Well, it got you here, didn't it?" she asked. "I'd say you came out the winner."

"Yes, I suppose you're right," I admitted. "But you've done pretty well for yourself."

She shrugged one shoulder, but she smiled as she did. "Would you gentlemen care for a drink?"

"Yes, please," I said.

For some reason known only to Chris, he suddenly rose from his seat and said, "I'm off to use the bathroom. Aft, is it?"

"Yes, sir," she answered, all the same. "Just inside the sixth compartment."

"Right," Chris said with a grunt, headed that way. A moment later, it was just me and her.

"As I was saying, can I get you anything?" She winked her blue eyes at me.

I ordered *Perrier* in ice.

"Are you sure you won't take anything with alcohol?" she asked. "After all, it's a long flight, and you might need something to help you sleep."

"Yes, I'm sure," I told her. "I need to stay sober."

She handed me my drink. "No problem. Here you go, dear."

"Thank you," I said.

"Do you mind if I sit for a minute?"

"No, go ahead," I told her.

She eased down next to me with a sigh, crossing her legs. "So, on your way to England?"

"Yes—"

"Going to fly for the British?"

I spit out my drink. "Where did you hear that?"

She cocked an eyebrow at me. "Come on, why else would you get a transfer to England?"

"Apparently, word has gone before me," I said dryly.

"Come on, dear, it's a small airplane," she said, pointing out.

"Okay, yeah," I said. "I've already been processed by the Clayton Knight Committee. I have my paperwork and everything."

"Why do you want to risk your life for the British?"

"This war is going to spread all over the world," I said, predicting what might happen. "It might seem far away right now, but eventually, America is going to get involved."

"I agree," she said calmly. "We can stick our heads in the sand all we want. It won't make the war go away."

I sat in silence, sipping my drink, glad to have met a like-minded person.

"Is there anything else I can do for you while your friend is in the head?"

"Really, that's not necessary," I told her.

"Are you sure? I won't get in trouble," she said coyly. "The other girls are at the other end of the airplane, tending to the family in the back."

"You mentioned head," I said.

"I might be persuaded," she said, glancing down. "After all, things might start to get a little too interesting for you in England. And I've liked you ever since you hopped off the mail plane, looking so scrumptious."

"Sounds good to me." I started to unzip my pants, but she stopped me.

"I'll get that, dear . . ."

A few minutes later, Cathy was fishing a tube of lipstick from her cart, fixing her smudged makeup. With a smile and wink in my direction, she pushed her cart into the next compartment. "Y'all will let me know if you need anything else?"

"Count on it," I told her.

A minute after that, Chris came back, plopping back down into the next couch. "So?" he asked in a breezy, airy, innocent tone that didn't fool me for a minute. "Did I miss anything?"

"Not a thing," I told him, in the same tone of voice. *Not unless you count an extraordinary blow job.*

"One thing's for sure . . . it's an eighteen-hour flight to Lisbon. What are we going to do?"

"Why do you think I brought a deck of cards?" I asked.

"Get them out," he said. "Let's kill some time."

"Might as well," I said.

"You got a quarter?" he asked me next. "We'll flip to start."

"Got one right here," I told him, putting my hand in my pocket to take out a quarter. It was a fairly old one, with the year 1931 on it.

What neither of us had the stones to mention was the reason why the plane was headed to Lisbon instead of another city — Portugal, like Spain and Sweden and the United States, had declared themselves neutral when hostilities had kicked off. Spain and Sweden would stay neutral throughout the entire war, but Portugal would shift its stance slightly, much like the United States would, allowing the creation of the Lend-Lease deal.

The quarter rose into the air, tumbling ass over tea kettle, and landed on *heads*. "Guess that means you start," I told Chris.

"Let's get started. Deal those cards."

After we got tired of using cards as a way to kill time, we both had paperback novels in our luggage.

CHAPTER THREE

Saturday, 2 March 1940

L ondon. We've finally arrived.
It's not quite as big as New York City in terms of population, but it's spread out all over the place instead of crammed in tight like New York.

The Clipper arrived in Lisbon very early in the morning, at which point we took a cab to the airport, where we caught a connecting flight to London, after signing a form that stated we understood that we would be flying into an active war zone.

Chris and I arrived in London about an hour later, at which point we got a hotel room and went to bed, grateful to be on solid ground once again. In the weeks and months to come, I was going to revisit the many and frequent visits Cathy gave in our compartment.

We had arrived very early in the morning, while it was still dark. It was a shock to see London completely blacked out – not a single light was visible. It's something the average New Yorker wasn't used to. I tried to visualize New York City blacked out and found it wasn't the same city. Guess that was the whole point.

Secretly, I wondered how in the hell the crew intended to land the plane when they couldn't even see where to go, but we weren't at the controls, so I did the most difficult thing I've ever done – I let others fly the plane. Monday morning, once we got some rest, we were headed straight to the nearest RAF Recruiting Office.

Monday morning, Chris and I walked down to the nearest Royal Air Force recruiting office in downtown London, which wasn't hard to find, and presented our processing paperwork to a young lady with blonde hair.

"You blokes are Americans?" She'd looked over our documents quite thoroughly.

"Yes," I said for the both of us. "We also have these."

I handed over our letters.

"Very good," she said, handing them back. "Let me make a phone call. You lot wait here."

"Yes, ma'am," I said.

In no time, an older officer came out to see us. He withdrew a faintly smoking briar pipe from his lips and said, "So, you chaps want to fly for us, eh?"

"Yes, sir," I told him.

The man had three stripes on each shoulder and spoke with a quiet, hard-won assurance. "Right then. I'm assuming you're staying in a hotel for the moment?"

"Yes, sir," I said.

"Not anymore," he told us. "Tomorrow morning at oh-six-hundred, there's a bus leaving for Middle Wallop. Be there with your bags. And don't be late. The bus won't wait. Any questions?"

"No, sir," we chorused.

"Good," he said. "And make sure you bring your paperwork."

"Yes, sir," I said.

Friday, 21 June 1940

Chris and I are now Pilot Officers in the Royal Air Force, a rank equal to second lieutenant, for which we're paid about 67 dollars a week in American money, a paltry sum compared to what I made at Pan Am. It was only later, much later, that I realized it was the first day of summer.

We've both spent the last couple of weeks at what the British called an Operational Training Unit. Now we're both due to find out where we're going to be posted. More later.

Just that morning we'd graduated from the final phase of our pilot training with an Operational Training Unit, finally getting to fly both *Spitfires* and *Hurricanes*. It had been the culmination of four months of training, starting on a chilly, damp March afternoon with induction into the Royal Air Force, taking a solemn, serious oath, at which point we became Officer Cadets.

The very next morning, we started four weeks of mandatory classroom instruction, learning about both the foundational aspects of flying a military plane and being an officer, including a protocol class on what to do if we ever met King George or Queen Elizabeth, both of whom visited the military regularly, the prospect of which *terrified* me. On top of all that, we started an intense regimen of daily physical activity.

Two days after induction, Chris and I were given dog tags. RAF dog tags were different from American ones. They were round instead of rectangular and hung from rope or cord instead of a ball chain. We were told to *never* take them off, not even to shower. After four months, I barely even noticed that I was wearing them anymore.

Once we'd finished classroom instruction, we started Elementary Flight Training in the first week of April, flying tame *Tiger Moth* biplanes, which, like overly gentle ponies, were just as scared of new pilots as they were of it. For Chris and I, however, mastering it was all too easy. We quickly grew bored of the *Tiger Moth* two-seater biplane with its simple, basic instruments, not to mention a *manual* starter—always a fun feature, especially on cold mornings. The manual starter meant that I or a ground crew member had to spin the propeller by hand until the engine caught and turned over. Sometimes, it took a few spins.

After about four weeks of Elementary Training, Chris and I soon graduated to Service Flight Training in the first week of May and to the *Miles Master*, a more advanced single-engine trainer that was at least an all-metal monoplane, sleek and modern, thanks to its single liquid-cooled inline engine which had an electric starter, thank God. I didn't tell my instructor that I'd already been flying such aircraft for *Pan Am*. But I jumped through the hoops required of me.

It was while we were learning the intricacies of flying the *Miles Master* that suddenly the war became all too real—and our training assumed a new urgency.

In the second weekend of May, the storm had finally broken—the Germans crossed the border into France and the Low Countries of western Europe. While the French at least had a military with which to defend its country, its government had been trying to convince itself, and its populace, that the war wasn't real and nothing was going to happen. The French were caught looking the other way. Even so, they put up quite a fight, especially with the British Expeditionary Force to help them out.

The same week as German air and ground forces were crossing the border into France, Neville Chamberlain faced a crisis in the form of a vote of *No Confidence* in the House of Commons, after which he was voted out and replaced by Winston Churchill. I'd been following events in the newspapers, wondering when the British would decide *enough was enough*. Chamberlain had appeased Hitler over and over again, letting him have his way in the interests of maintaining the peace, only to find out Hitler wasn't playing by the same rules.

By the last week of May, however, the combined British and French forces had been pushed back to the tiny village of Dunkirk on the French coast along the English Channel, where they waited for the Germans to finish the job. For reasons known only to the German general in command, they also decided to wait, allowing the British a chance to rescue their stranded troops.

In the space of about a week, coinciding with a rare period of calm seas in the English Channel, the British made use of every small ship they could find — Royal Navy destroyers, ferry ships, tugboats, fishing trawlers, and even sailboats. By the time all was said and done, Operation Dynamo was a smashing success. A combined total estimate of 330,000 British and French troops had been evacuated to fight again another day.

Chris and I had just graduated from five weeks of Service Flight Training, getting our wings and our rank, Pilot Officer, equivalent to Second Lieutenant, and were posted to an Operational Training Unit in the first week of June. If I concentrated hard enough, I could almost feel the extra weight from that measly half-stripe on my sleeves, as well as the pilot wings on my left breast pocket. By the time we'd graduated from Operational Unit Training, the Germans were massing their aircraft at airfields all across northern France.

As Churchill himself had said on the radio, "The Battle of France is over. I expect the Battle of Britain is about to begin."

The Germans were planning an invasion of England, codenamed Operation Sea Lion. In order to mount that invasion, they had to establish air superiority over the Channel and England itself. And, to do that, they had to neutralize the Royal Air Force, as well as impact the British ability to make the tools of war.

According to reports, the Luftwaffe had more than two *thousand* aircraft to throw at us across the Channel — bombers and single-engine fighters mostly, but also dive bombers and heavy twin-engine fighters.

The Royal Air Force, on the other hand, had about seven *hundred* fighter planes to counter this — a mix of *Hawker Hurricanes* and *Supermarine Spitfires* — three to one odds. But we had a secret weapon that nobody else had that wasn't even technically a weapon—radar. In the spring of 1940, it was brand-new. Nobody else had it. I'd say that made the odds even.

But that was just part of it. In addition to radar, there was a network of observers, with radios and telephones, which had direct communication with sector stations. From these sector stations, they could direct entire air battles. It was called the *Dowding Method*, in honor of the man who invented it—Hugh Dowding, commander of RAF Fighter Command.

Chris and I were about to find out our fates. On a sparkling, cloudless afternoon in June, four months later, Chris and I were reporting to the office where new pilots went to find out where they were being posted.

We were both hoping to get postings to the Eleven Group sector, where the action was going to be heaviest. I'd had the good sense to not tell my folks back home what I was really doing, and instead I told them about the boring flights the airline had me taking. They believed me. I think they did, anyway.

Meanwhile, we walked into the *Personnel Despatch Centre*, a rather large, busy office tucked away in a corner of the base, and snapped to attention, saluting smartly as we introduced ourselves.

"Stand by a moment, chaps," the officer in charge said, a serious, middle-aged officer with three stripes on each shoulder, wearing an RAF-blue sweater over a shirt and tie instead of a jacket, a pipe stuck in between his teeth. "Jane, my dear?"

"Yes, sir?" A brunette lady looked up from her desk.

"You have the posting orders for our two young men?"

"Yes, sir," she said, rising from her desk to open a file drawer.

She riffled through the drawer for a few moments, pausing only to extract two single-page letters, and handed them to her boss. A moment later, he handed them to us. Looking at my letter, I saw it had been typed on yellow paper, was short, tersely worded, and got straight to the point.

"*Ten* Group?" I said, looking up, not believing it. According to the letter, I was being posted to RAF Exeter, an airfield a short, ten-minute flight from the southern coast, part of Ten Group—well away from London and the main thrust of the action. I looked at Chris. "What about you?"

"Me, too," he said, holding up his own letter. "Ten Group."

I turned back to the posting officer, considering how to say what I wanted to say, but he beat me to the punch.

"Ten Group. You're welcome," the officer said in a blunt, matter of fact tone, removing his pipe from his mouth. "Although if it's action you chaps are craving, I expect the Luftwaffe will be all too willing to throw you a bone."

I swallowed down my initial reply. Instead, I just said, "Thank you, sir."

"Get your bags packed," he told us next. "Enjoy your last civilized meal this evening. The bus for Exeter leaves tomorrow morning at oh-seven-thirty. Do take care out there, lads."

"Yes, sir," we chorused, saluting as one man.

He reeled off a return salute. "Dismissed."

As we walked off, headed towards the barracks to pack our things, Chris said, "Not too late to back out, you know."

"Are you kidding me? You're not getting cold feet, are you?"

He was quiet for a long time before he said, "I'd be lying if I said no. You gotta admit, the odds are not in our favor."

Now I was quiet, thinking a bit before I replied, "We've come this far. I'm not about to desert, not right before I get posted to a real squadron."

Chris nodded several times. "I thought you'd say that," he told me. "Come on, let's go pack."

"Right."

Saturday, 22 June 1940

Chris and I got our orders yesterday after four long months of training. This morning, we boarded a bus for our first duty posting – RAF Exeter, an airfield a ten-minute flight away from the south coast of England along the English Channel, five minutes away by motor car from the town of Exeter.

By the time Chris and I had graduated from Operational Unit Training, the Germans had completed their conquest of France. The same week we finished Operational Unit Training, the French were signing the formal surrender in the same subway car where the Armistice ending the First World War was signed.

Now it's all for real.

The war was waiting, just across the English Channel. When would it come over?

After a two-hour drive south from Middle Wallop that morning, Chris and I got off the bus along with a few others, stretching our legs as we did, and formed a line to be greeted by a bustling, busy airfield. When we left Middle Wallop, the morning had been cool and misty. By the time we'd arrived at RAF Exeter, it had turned into a warm, sunny day. Directly across from us was a small building with a sign saying *Aircrew Reception Centre*.

Just behind was a wrought iron gate framed by tall trees, with a guard shack to one side. Standing in front was a small group of people.

Chris and I found out later that no less than five fighter squadrons called Exeter home, three of *Hurricanes* and two of *Spitfires*. I was desperately hoping that I would get posted to one of the *Spitfire* squadrons, but as the saying goes, beggars couldn't be choosers.

No sooner had we formed a line than a small group of of-

ficers addressed us. Speaking for the group was a female officer with platinum-blonde hair and a no-nonsense manner
about her.

"All right, there," she said. "My name is Leftenant Kate
Stroud. I'm the Group Quartermaster. I'll be giving you your
postings. Then I'll hand you off to your respective Squadron
Leaders. Have your files ready. Right then." And she started
calling off names in rapid fashion.

"Cooper, Matthew!"

"Here," I said.

"Don't just stand there, come over here," she snapped.

Suppressing a grin, I marched over to her and saluted
smartly, my file tucked under my arm. "Ma'am."

"Wipe that stupid grin off your face, pilot," she said, only
slightly less snappily. "This is serious."

"Yes, ma'am," I said, attempting to put on a straight face,
noticing her eyes were ice-blue.

"Right then," she said, consulting a list. "Your Squadron
Leader is Michael Higgins."

At that moment, another officer stepped up, middle-aged,
wearing the two-and-a-half stripes of a Squadron Leader and
a serious though friendly expression, a clump of wheat-colored hair on his head. Removing his hands from behind his
back, he stepped up, hand extended. "Welcome to three-oh-
one Squadron."

"Thank you, sir," I said, taking his hand.

"Americans, eh?"

"Yes, sir," I said. No sense in denying it. "Although, you
might want to keep it to yourself."

He winked. "Quite so. Don't worry. To us, you're Cana-
dian."

"Thank you, sir."

"We're ruddy thrilled to have you, chaps," he said. "I'm
waiting for your fellow American to join us. Then we can

head over to our squadron area."

"Yes, sir," I said.

One sad effect of Germany's conquest of Europe was that surviving pilots from the air forces of the conquered nations had made their way to the United Kingdom to fly for the Royal Air Force. As a result, the RAF was one of the most diverse air forces in the world in June 1940, with pilots from all over Europe and all over the world serving in it, including Americans.

It took the better part of ten minutes for the female officer to make it through her list, but eventually, Chris came to join me. I was glad. If nothing else, I would have a familiar face to look at.

"Nice going," I told him in a low voice.

"Thanks," he said in the same tone. "Although I can't take any credit."

"You lot have your files?" Higgins asked.

"Right here, sir," I said as I handed them over.

"Come on, this way," Higgins said, gesturing for Chris and I to follow as he took our paperwork.

We followed Higgins through the gate and some ways across a grass field that had been turned into an improvised runway, thanks to a series of pierced steel planks, which had been laid down on the grass, stretching from one end of the runway all the way to the other end.

On the near side were trees, the reception committee, and the entry gate, while on the far side of the runway were airplanes, dozens of airplanes, both *Hurricanes* and *Spitfires*, most painted dark green with dark brown stripes, but some painted dark grey with dark green stripes, all parked in front of enormous aircraft hangars.

Apart from the huge aircraft hangars, sitting close to the runway was a tiny house with a small sign that I couldn't quite read from this distance.

The two planes, the *Hawker Hurricane* and *Supermarine Spitfire*, were easily distinguished from each other. *Spitfires* had a frameless bubble canopy with a side door, allowing ground crew to assist with strapping the pilot in, as well as a distinctive wing shape. Its eight *Browning* machine guns were evenly spaced out along its wings. *Hurricanes*, on the other hand, had a framed canopy. Its lines weren't quite as sexy and streamlined as the *Spitfire's* were, its eight guns, four on each wing, bunched together instead of spread out. The *Hawker Hurricane* was more like a Plain Jane than a Marlene Deitrich, but it could be refueled and rearmed in less than ten minutes, meaning a squadron of *Hurricanes* could be ready for action in about two hours, while the *Spitfire* required almost half an hour for each plane, meaning a squadron took more than five hours to be refueled and rearmed.

The one feature the two planes had in common was their engines—the liquid-cooled inline *Merlin* piston engine from *Rolls-Royce*, which generated more than 1,000 horsepower at the time, thanks to 100-octane aviation fuel from America. Development over the war would yield yet more powerful engines delivering additional horsepower.

It still remained to be seen which planes we would be flying—*Hurricanes* or *Spitfires*—two of the finest fighter planes in the world. I still wanted to be flying a *Spitfire*, but as I said, beggars couldn't be choosers. I was checked out on either one. I would've been happy flying either one.

After a walk of several minutes, we finally arrived at the far end of the runway, stopping only at the tiny house with a simple sign out front that read *Dispersal*.

Inside the house was a fully functional office, including a telephone off in the corner. At yet another desk, a young lady sat before a typewriter, her auburn hair up in a bun, her fingers daintily working the keys, absorbed in her work.

"Come on in," Higgins told us, taking a seat behind a desk,

placing our files on the desktop. "Have a seat, lads."

We quickly did so.

Higgins glanced again at our files before he handed them to a second female subordinate, who asked, "Shall I file these, sir?"

"Yes, please."

"Yes, sir."

"Thank you, Mary."

Then he turned to us and continued, "My name is Squadron Leader Michael Higgins. You can call me Higgins or just sir is fine."

"Yes, sir," I said.

"Now, in case you were not made aware, this is the dispersal hut of not just three-oh-one Squadron, but for the whole base. Either myself or another squadron leader will always stand watch. That phone over there will only ring for one reason. When or if it does, you're to drop whatever you're doing. If the air raid sirens start going off, drop what you're doing and take cover. Clear?"

"Crystal," I said.

"Good. As I was saying, I'm quite thrilled to have you," he said. "So far, it's been quiet, dreadfully so, but I don't expect that to continue for much longer. I'll have someone take you over to your tent shortly. Take the rest of the day to get settled in. Sometime today, I'll introduce you to the rest of the squadron, then tomorrow you'll start. I expect you chaps have completed Operational Unit Training?"

"Yes, sir," I said for the both of us.

"Jolly good," he said with a hearty tone. "I'm sorry we don't have the chance to get you familiarized, but time is short, and I'm afraid you'll have to hit the ground running."

"Suits us, sir," I said. "We've been through enough training."

He grunted. Then he smiled as someone entered the house.

"Ah, good. There you are."

"You called for me, sir?"

"Yes, indeed. Gentlemen, this is Devon."

We turned to see a young brunette girl standing at attention, hair pinned up in a tight bun, wearing RAF blue and low-heeled shoes, two stripes on each sleeve denoting her a Corporal. After a moment, we turned back to our new squadron leader, whose smile was still in place.

"As I was saying, this is Devon. She'll be showing you where you're going to sleep. When the sun rises, so do you. When the sun sets, our day is over. Copy that?"

"Loud and clear, sir," I said for the both of us.

"Good. Go get settled in. I expect I'll see you later. Devon, please show them where they sleep."

"Yes, sir," the brunette said. "Come with me, loves."

"What about our bags?" I asked her.

"Don't worry, they've already been taken over," she told us. "Let us know if you need anything else. In case you forgot anything."

"Thank you," I said.

"Not at all," she said, continuing to stride along.

We had to work hard to keep up with the young lady, who, we both noted, was hardly even breathing hard. But we were both up to the task of keeping up with her.

Just a few minutes later we arrived at a large tent located near a grove of trees well back from the flight line, in which there sat six cots, each with its own footlocker, and were led in turn to the two empty beds, each with an empty foot locker, each foot locker with a padlock and a key on top.

Our bags had been placed on our respective cots.

"Here are your beds," she said in a matter-of-fact tone. "As I said before, let me know if you need anything."

"Thank you," we said. Then I asked her, "What's your

name?"

"Corporal Devon Buxton, sir," she answered promptly.

"Are you from Exeter?"

"No, sir," she answered. "But from the area."

"I see," I said.

"Will there be anything else?" she asked.

"No, that will be all," I told her with a casual salute. "You're dismissed."

"Very good," she said. With a single, crisp nod, she saluted, pivoted smartly, and marched away.

"Well, what have we here?"

I turned. A young, tall man stood there. He looked nineteen, maybe twenty years old if he was a day, with an unruly mop of dark hair on his head. His eyes were dark blue and sparkled with humor.

"Flying Officer Vern Holliday," he said, introducing himself. "Sprogs?"

I'd heard the term before. It simply meant recruits or newbies. "Yes," I said, introducing ourselves. "Just arrived today. I'm Matt Cooper, and this is Chris Edwards."

We shook hands. "Lovely to meet you chaps," he said. "Americans, eh?"

"Yes," we both said.

"Great to have you," he told us. "Met the Old Man?"

"Yes," I said. "Higgins seems solid."

Holliday cracked a grin. "That describes him to a *T*."

I met his grin with my own. If nothing else, I had a good read of what sort of fellow our squadron leader was.

"Seen any action yet?" Chris asked.

"Some of us have already," Holliday answered. "Covering the Dunkirk evacuation."

"Things have quieted down since then," I said with a glum tone.

"Indeed they have," Holliday said. "But don't worry, that

won't stay the same for long."

"Thanks," I told him, getting tired of hearing polite variations of *we just don't know*. It was the oldest story in the military—hurry up and wait—no matter what branch you were in.

After a long moment, I asked Chris, "Which bed you want?"

Once we'd decided that, I asked Holliday, "Which way is the bathroom? And when's dinner? We haven't had a bite to eat since breakfast."

Holliday chuckled. "No problem," he told me. "You lot follow me."

"After you," I said.

"Stay close to me," he told us. "Come along, I'll show you where the bog is."

Once Holliday had shown us the layout of the place—including where the bathroom was, which was actually a ditch—we saw to moving our meager things into our respective foot lockers. That took us about ten minutes, sadly enough. After that, we had a chance to meet the rest of the guys, as well as a few of the guys from the other *Spitfire* squadron—204 Squadron. That took the rest of the day. A few hours later, we got a visitor.

"Uh-ten-*hut!*"

We all snapped to attention. A profound wave of relief swept through me when I saw it was Higgins, our squadron leader. Earlier that day, we'd met The Brass—Wing Commander Quimby, in charge of both *Spitfire* squadrons, as well as Group Captain Nigel Holmes, the base commander.

"Well, I see you chaps have gotten your things moved in."

"Yes, sir," we answered.

"Jolly good," he said. "You two, come with me."

Wondering what that was about, we dutifully followed

him out of the tent and across the base, which was fairly easy to do since he was walking quick but not too fast. As we walked, I couldn't help but notice how far the sun had sunk in the west. It was amazing how fast the day had gone.

I soon realized we were headed back to the flight line. Dozens of aircraft sat waiting for some unknown signal. Pilots either sat lounging about, reading, or playing soccer — excuse me, football, as it was called here in England. I was still getting used to that.

"All right, Cooper," he told me. "Here's our squadron area. You can tell because our Dispersal hut is right over there." He pointed.

"Okay," I said.

"And here is our aircraft."

Feeling like a kid at Christmas, I saw the *Spitfires*. "Uhm, so which one is mine, sir?"

Higgins cracked a boyish grin, clapping me on the arm. "Come along. This way."

I followed him as he jauntily walked further along till he stopped at a certain *Spitfire*, with the letters *T YV* prominently painted on the fuselage, between the main wing and the tail section, on either side of the roundel, the big national emblem of England, somewhat resembling an archery target, and ahead of the aircraft serial number. *YV* was the squadron code, while the single *T* designated the aircraft, which was painted dark green with dark brown stripes, while the underside was painted light blue, the letters on the fuselage painted in black. At the very end of the fuselage, right before the tail rudder, was a single white stripe with black letters painted over it. That was the aircraft serial number, in this case *TH138*.

She was beautiful. And she was mine. I just knew I had a big-ass grin plastered all over my face. Higgins squeezed my shoulder and moved off to find Chris.

A moment later, I felt a different hand on my shoulder. "So

what do you think?"

It was Holliday. "She's beautiful," I said, voicing my thoughts, and I meant it.

"I love the *Spitfire*," he told me, gazing at the plane himself. "She's a sweet-handling bird."

"Aye, indeed she is," I said, using a Brit phrase.

"Treat her right, and she'll always bring you home."

"Yes, sir," I said, recognizing sage advice when I heard it.

A moment later, Chris joined us. "Did you get yours?"

"Sure did," I said. "That one."

"Nice," he said.

"What about you?" I asked.

"That one over there," he said, pointing.

"Way to go, pal," I told him.

Chris turned to Holliday. "Too bad we don't have any bubbly to celebrate, sir."

Holliday cracked a grin, making his eyes crinkle. "I might be persuaded to find some," he said cagily. "I could use a drink after dinner myself, which is in about an hour. After that, we'll be knocking off, so it's safe."

"Sounds good to me," I said. Raising my arms, I wrapped each arm around my squadron-mates' shoulders and said, "This is going to be fun."

Just as he'd said, once the sun had set and we were free to knock off for the evening, we had our evening meal, for which Chris and I were grateful as it was the first meal we'd had all day, after which we retired to our tent for a nightcap, opening that bottle of bubbly.

It tasted good. Brotherhood and fellowship made it taste even better.

I revisited that night many times in the next few weeks, the last moments of calm before the storm washed up on our shores.

Chapter Four

Sunday, 23 June 1940

Well, it's official. Chris and I got our orders. Yesterday, we left Middle Wallop after having spent four months there and boarded a bus for RAF Exeter. Once there, we spent the rest of the day settling in and getting to know the boys of 301 Squadron, just one of five squadrons based here.

They're a jolly bunch of guys, ready to give their lives in defense of their nation. I was both honored and humbled to be in their company. I'm not sure how Chris felt, but judging by the look on his face when we got our aircraft yesterday, I'd say he feels the same.

We awoke with the rising of the sun.

The war was waiting. Time to join the party.

Even though we officially started the next day, Sunday, Chris and I weren't called up until Thursday morning. The sun hadn't properly risen yet as we headed out of our tent for breakfast. Mist still hung on, and although the day promised to be warm and sunny, the mist was rapidly clearing.

"All right, there."

Chris and I were still waking up, although the Royal Air Force coffee was strong, helping out with that, at five in the frickin morning. *Damn.* "Good morning, sir," I said.

"You have a mission for us, sir?" Chris asked.

"Indeed, I do," he said, speaking in a grave tone. "Come over here." He led us to a map spread out across a table. "I need you three to patrol the Channel, flying along this vector, like so."

He took a ruler and drew a line with a pencil.

I nodded my understanding.

"Your mission is merely to scout the area. If you find *anything*, get back here straight away to report what you saw. Your knowledge doesn't do us any good if we never get it."

"Understood," we said.

"Good," he said. "Where's Holliday?"

"Right here, sir," a male voice replied.

I turned. Holliday was standing there. I waved at him. He waved back.

"You heard all that?"

"Every word, sir," he said in a reassuring tone.

"I'm counting on it," he told us. "Now, get moving. Your aircraft are waiting."

"Yes, sir," we chorused, saluting as one man.

"Dismissed," he told us, returning the salute.

The three of us jogged over to the flight line, where our *Spitfires* had been moved onto the runway. The engines of all three already started, turning over with a cough of exhaust. Since the three of us were already suited up over our battle dress uniforms, in leather helmets, goggles, Mae West inflation vest, and parachute harness, all we had to do was climb into our aircraft.

As I climbed on the left wing of my *Spitfire*, I felt a powerful mix of pride, anxiety, and adrenaline. *It was finally going to happen.*

That was my main thought as I climbed in. Holding on to the windscreen with one hand and the canopy with the other, I eased down and parked my butt, reassured by the instrument panel as the crew chief helped me strap on the aircraft. Dead ahead at eye level on the dashboard was the gunsight, a single yellow ring with crosshairs, projected on a glass plate. Right away, I grabbed the control stick, topped by a metal ring that housed a red button, and moved it, testing the plane's control surfaces. After a moment, the crew chief gave me a thumbs-up.

Then he closed the side door, patted it, and said, "Good hunting, sir!"

I didn't reply but gave him a jaunty salute.

Sliding the canopy shut, he hopped off the wing, running off to the side.

One at a time, Holliday first, we went roaring down the runway, lifting off into the clear morning sky, headed due south for the coast.

Just a few minutes later, we were at angels-ten, meaning ten thousand feet of altitude, flying along our assigned vector. Once we'd climbed to altitude and were above the clouds, it was a bright, glorious, sunny day. High, thin cirrus clouds were the only thing spoiling the blue sky. The three of us were flying a tight triangular formation called a Vic or just a V because, from the ground, it looked just like the letter V upside down.

Holliday came on the radio. "You two with me?"

"We're on your six," I said.

"Good. Let's keep to our vector and see if we can find anything. Remember the mission."

"Yes, sir," I said.

"And one more thing. If either of you see your low fuel state light come on, call out *Bingo Fuel*, and we all return to base. Copy that?"

"Loud and clear," I replied.

"Very good," Holliday said. "Now, let's see if we can find anything."

It was amazing to me how something could be both exciting *and* boring at the same time, but that's how my first patrol went.

It was exciting in the sense that it was my first official mission as a pilot for the Royal Air Force, but the mission itself was anything but—flying out to a certain distance over the English Channel along a certain heading and back to home base again, always on the lookout for anything suspicious, up to and including enemy activity or sightings of it.

With the English Channel far below us like a glittering plate of glass and blue sky above, it was hard to concentrate on this idyllic summer day, and I reminded myself there was a war on, and I was on a mission. But concentrate I did.

Once I saw what I thought was a German destroyer searching for convoys, but Holliday took a look and told me it was just a Royal Navy destroyer.

"Sorry," I told him.

"Don't be sorry," he replied. "Good looking out. Keep looking. There's probably a convoy nearby."

"Roger that," I said.

The rest of the patrol passed uneventfully.

More than an hour later, we landed at Exeter, where we found out we hadn't been the only patrol sent out that morning. Most of the patrols turned up nothing, like mine, while others had located vital convoys inbound across the Channel.

After we'd returned to base, we'd been debriefed. Then Higgins took our reports and attended a meeting with the brass. He returned to the Dispersal hut an hour later with news. Our base and every squadron in it now had a new mission—air cover of friendly convoys. If a convoy called for air cover, well, you know the rest.

We start our new mission on Monday.

The war was coming closer, whether I wanted it to or not. I wasn't sure how I felt about that. I did know that I sure as hell wasn't going to write home about it.

After all, they thought I was still flying for *Pan Am*.

CHAPTER FIVE

Thursday, 11 July 1940

It's official. The war is here.
My squadron has new orders — to give air cover to convoys and make sure the ships actually make port. It was almost a sure bet that the Germans would go after our convoys. We've been on alert for about a week now. We only had to sit and wait, which was the worst part. But the Luftwaffe would come calling soon enough. Just a matter of when.

Chris and I have been accepted into the squadron. We sleep in a tent with four other pilots. Man, do they snore, but they're friendly enough. I find it odd, however, that we haven't had any hot scramble drills. Maybe they want to conserve the fuel?

We're only waiting for the phone in Dispersal to ring.

The first week of July had been beautiful, just like this week — warm, sunny, pleasant days and mild nights — or would have been without the war.

Today was spent just like the last several days, lounging about on pool recliners with full flying kit, ready to go, reading, and talking while some of the guys kicked a football between them.

So far, the day had been a crushing bore. The morning was turning into a bright, hot summer afternoon as Chris and I sat in our chairs.

Next to me, Chris yawned.

"You know that's contagious," I said to him.

Chris chuckled but didn't reply.

Quite suddenly, with no warning at all — the phone in Dispersal rang. The loud, strident sound carried easily through the hazy afternoon air. When it did, the soccer ball was forgotten. It rolled across the grass and gently bumped against a tree.

Chris and I sat up straight and tall in our chairs to listen.

Higgins picked up the receiver. "Dispersal . . . Right." He hung up. Then he barked out, "You lot! *Move!* We got two squadrons inbound over the Channel headed for a convoy! Go!"

We went for our ships at a dead run, where ground crew were already turning engines over with coughs of exhaust, then, once the engines were started, disconnected the starter carts.

Moments later, I climbed on the wing of my *Spitfire* and plopped down in the seat while the crew chief helped me strap on the airplane. Then, as before, he closed the side door, slid the canopy closed, and gave it a pat. The wheel chocks were removed, and the crew ran to the side.

Not even until the day I died was I going to forget that first hot scramble. Our squadron went roaring down the runway at full throttle, two or three planes at a time, clawing our way into the air.

The *Spitfires* went off first, followed by a squadron of *Hurricanes* behind ours, lifting off into the afternoon sky.

Twenty minutes later, we were at twenty thousand feet, flying through a bank of clouds, and I was fighting a sense of growing impatience, wondering when the idiot flight controllers back on dry land would set us loose.

I'd discovered through listening to radio chatter that our squadron callsign was *Ivy*, which was fitting, considering the squadron letters of *VY*. Right at the moment, we were flying in a stair-step formation, all fifteen of us, five flights of three, the lead flight at the top of the stairs, while I was in the last flight at the bottom. I knew Chris was nearby.

The squadron of *Hurricanes* was somewhere behind us.

Even though impatience was burning a hole in the back of my mind, I made myself follow orders. Then I made myself relax as I realized the sun was directly behind me, and we were being carefully vectored in, wasting time and precious fuel but being vectored in.

Right at that moment, we flew out of that bank of clouds — and there they were.

The enemy!

I felt a big jolt of adrenaline shoot through me.

They were flying two separate formations, one squadron of single-engine *BF-109*, escorting a second squadron of twin-engine *BF-110's*.

And far below was the convoy, about sixty defenseless ships.

"Tally-*ho!*" I crowed. "Bandits, lots of bandits, one o'clock low!"

"Good looking out, Cooper," Higgins said. "But we can't go yet."

A second voice came on, that of the leader of the other squadron, flying *Hurricanes*. "There they are. Ivy, you lot take the fighters. We'll go for the bombers."

"You heard him," Higgins told us. "Let's go!"

Without a second thought, I rolled my *Spitfire* over, peeled off, and dove for the formation of German fighters.

In the virgin skies over the English Channel, the fighting began.

The moment we came diving out of the sun, the two squadrons scattered like leaves on the wind.

We did likewise, chasing after the German fighter planes.

I was trying to get a bead on one *Messerschmitt* when I heard, "Cooper, *move!* You've got a bandit on your tail!"

Without even thinking, I rolled my *Spitfire* over on its side and turned as tightly as I dared. A moment later, the *Messerschmitt* roared past, a flash of color and sound. Again, without thinking, I rolled back the other way and got on his tail.

A moment later, I had him in my sights. I squeezed the trigger without hesitation.

The first hundred rounds or so in my guns were tracer rounds — they were painted phosphorous so they were easily visible as they flew through the air. But with eight guns, four in each wing, the tracer rounds didn't last long. However, I didn't fire long, either, only a few seconds, in fact, before I saw a huge fireball erupt from the engine. The enemy plane plunged into the sea, trailing dense black smoke. I didn't see anyone bail out.

"Good job, Cooper," Higgins said.

"Thank you, sir," I said, the adrenaline pumping through me.

The rat race continued for several more minutes with me trying to repeat that feat, but much to my disappointment, no German fighter jock was willing to fall for it again.

Right after that, someone called out, "Bingo fuel!"

So Higgins said, "That's it, lads. Knock it off and return to base."

As we formed up to return to Exeter, I looked at the clock on my instrument panel and was stunned to see the whole thing had taken just *five minutes*.

During the flight back, my own *Low Fuel* light winked on.

We landed back at home base minutes later with practically dry fuel tanks. I'd had just enough fuel to land and taxi off the runway. My prop stopped turning before I cut the engine off.

But what happened next was worse.

I slipped the straps off, climbed out of the airplane, staggered over to the closest tree, collapsed onto all fours, and threw up all over the grass. The adrenaline rush had faded. Now, the shaking had taken over. Embarrassed was the least of how I felt.

Then I felt a hand on my shoulder. I looked up to see Higgins. I quickly rose to stand at awkward attention. "Sir."

"That's all right, lad," he said, his voice quiet and sympathetic. "It happens to everyone after their first mission."

"Yes, sir," I said, gaining more control over myself.

"Come on, we have to debrief with the Group Intel lads. Let's go."

"Yes, sir."

About four hours later, once the after-action reports had been typed up and taken to the brass, I found myself with one confirmed kill — and awarded a Distinguished Flying Cross for my trouble. A swastika symbol would be painted on my aircraft, just under the canopy. Later that week, there was going to be a ceremony where the group captain, wing commander, and the squadron leader, Higgins, would pin the medal on my chest and take turns shaking my hand.

"Nice work, Cooper," Higgins told me. "Not many pilots score their first kill their first time out."

"Thank you, sir," I said.

"Keep this up, and at this rate, you could be an ace," he said.

"Really?"

"Yes. And I think you've earned this," he said, opening a desk drawer and pulling out a metal flask. He unscrewed the top and handed it to me. "Brandy," he explained. "For your nerves. Cheers." He took a slug, then handed it to me.

"Thank you, sir." Without a second thought, I took a slug.

It was only after I'd swallowed the alcohol that I realized

I'd just broken about half a dozen regs, but I also figured it was just as well. It would take a couple more hours to refuel and rearm our squadron.

In a daze, I returned to the lounge chairs by the runway. But once I sat down, a curious thing happened. I just wanted to sit there and do absolutely zero—just sit there and do nothing, say nothing, not lift so much as an eyebrow, and meld to the chair.

For a brief moment, I panicked when I noticed Chris wasn't there, but a moment later, he plopped down in the chair next to mine and did the same thing, just sat there.

"Good to see you, pal," I told him.

"We made it," he said.

"Hate to burst your bubble, blokes, but that was just your first mission," Holliday said as he came to join us a minute later.

"Thanks," Chris said in a dry tone.

Holliday cracked a grin. "Just keeping it on the real," he said. "But like Higgins said, you two did brilliantly on your first mission. In fact, it was wizard."

That meant good. Really good.

"Thanks," we both said this time.

"In the meantime," he said, settling down into his own chair. "We can relax. It'll be a couple hours yet before our planes are ready to go. By that time, it'll be time to knock off."

CHAPTER SIX

Monday, 12 August 1940

Over the last month or so, the action has been steadily, if slowly, ramping up, with the Luftwaffe putting up more frequent air strikes against shipping in the Channel. I'm trying not to begrudge the pace. Eleven Group's fighter squadrons have been scrambling much more often than us. There have been days when we've been scrambled twice in one day, followed by several days where we weren't sent out at all, or sent out once in a day.

July went fast at that rate. Now, it was August – the dog days of summer.

I said as much to Higgins, our squadron leader, who then told me that in August, the battle would only heat up from here, much like the weather. Personally, I welcomed a potential increase in the action. Although, I also knew that the Luftwaffe was going to get serious about taking us out.

The Luftwaffe's mission was simple – to wear us down so that we were no longer an effective fighting force.

Nobody knew when it would start – except soon, or so I was told. Sometime in August.

Until then . . . we wait.

Nothing happened all week until it was Thursday, the fifteenth of August. For some reason, I had a vague premonition of dread that morning the moment I sat up in my cot and stretched.

Something was going to happen.

My grandmother Mabel, as well as my mom and my sister,

Veronica, were all given to having these premonitions, or *funny feelings*, as Grandma called them. I thought I'd been spared, but apparently, such was not the case.

The bad feeling persisted even as we lined up to get morning rations, also called breakfast, and coffee. My stomach rumbled unpleasantly at me, the cost of all this tension-filled waiting. July had been plenty exciting all on its own, but then, for some reason, the action cut way down over the last few days. That made me more uneasy than anything, especially when I saw how it made the brass, who'd looked worried.

Having the battle take place over England itself instead of out over the Channel was both good and bad—good because it meant that the German fighter planes would be at the ragged edge of their range, with just ten minutes of fuel left before they had to turn back for home. If any of us got shot down, we would get to bail out over friendly territory, but also bad, because, of course, now the Luftwaffe would be striking targets on home turf. I'd been wanting the war to come to me. Now it was here.

We'd barely had a chance to digest our breakfast, suit up, and take our customary seats by the runway—when the phone rang. Chris and I sat bolt upright, as several other guys did.

Higgins answered. "Dispersal." All at once, he hung up. "You lot! We got a big one! Let's go!"

Once again, we ran out to our aircraft. We were airborne in minutes.

That premonition was stronger than ever as we climbed to altitude. On this day, there were fewer clouds to fly through. However, I couldn't help but notice *four* squadrons had been scrambled, two each of *Hurricanes* and *Spitfires*. I could see the two squadrons of *Hurricanes* off to my left. Obviously, this was going to be big.

Just as before, however, we were being vectored in.

All at once, we broke into the clear — and there they were, laid out before us like a picture postcard, a formation of about fifty German bombers, all of them *Heinkels* with streamlined fuselages, twin engines, and slightly swept-back wings, painted dark gray on top with bright yellow on their engine cowlings. Most unusually, I couldn't see any fighter escorts, and I wondered if they were hanging back or maybe they got lost on the way to the party.

This time, I held my tongue, watching them from behind my oxygen mask.

One of the other squadron leaders came on. "All right, I don't see any fighter escorts. Everybody, let's do some damage, but watch out for any escorts."

"You heard the man, ladies," Higgins told us. "Let's go!"

Without any hesitation, I rolled my *Spitfire* over, peeled off, and dove for the formation.

Twenty minutes later, we were back at base. This time, I didn't throw up, but I also couldn't help but notice that uneasy feeling was still with me. That thought kept lingering in the back of my mind while we were debriefed, but I didn't tell anybody about it — until Higgins said to me, "Cooper, you notice anything strange about this raid?"

The Group Intel boys had already left. I'd been the last pilot in our squadron to be debriefed.

"The size of it, mainly," I said. "Fifty planes, give or take."

"Very good," he said. "Anything else?"

"Unless I was very much mistaken, they were headed in our general direction. That or another of the airfields along the coast."

"Yes," he said, sounding concerned. "I'm meeting with the other squadron leaders. I'll see if their lads noticed the same thing. In the meantime, good work. That's your second confirmed kill."

"Thank you, sir," I said.

I'd shot down a single enemy bomber, earning my second confirmed kill, and managed to score a *damaged* before my *Low Fuel* light winked on, which meant a return to base.

The afternoon was turning into early evening, around five-thirty or so, according to my watch, when the phone rang again. Once again, everybody stopped what they were doing to listen.

"Everybody!" Higgins shouted. "There's a raid headed straight for us! Move!"

Less than five minutes later, we went roaring down the runway, me doing several things at once, like retracting the undercarriage, trimming the flaps, and sliding the canopy into place. In all that flurry of activity, I forgot about my bad feeling. But once things settled down, it came roaring back.

It turned out the raid wasn't headed for Exeter after all, but Middle Wallop instead, which made little difference to the pilots in the air, whose mission was to stop the enemy or make them turn back, no matter what the target was. If anything, Middle Wallop was the bigger target because it was a training base, as well as a major sector station for Ten Group.

In any case, it didn't take long once we were in the air to meet the formation of bombers as they were crossing the coast, on course for Middle Wallop. On this otherwise idyllic summer day, the cloud cover was heavy, but once we climbed high enough, we were literally above it all, although we kept drifting in and out of cloud cover.

By this time, I'd learned to trust the ground controllers. Somehow, they always knew where the sun was at. They always vectored us in so that we had the sun at our backs, which meant that when we attacked, it was out of the sun.

As we kept flying through clouds, I kept thinking we were going to miss them. But then, all at once, we flew out of the clouds into the clear blue sky, and I saw them—two squadrons each of twin-engine bombers and single-engine fighters.

As the British would say, Bloody hell. This was going to be *Big*.

At that moment, the sun was directly behind us, so I knew the moment was coming.

Sure enough, just as we emerged from the clouds, all four squadrons, one of the *Hurricane* squadron leaders said, "There they are. We'll take the bombers. You lot in the *Spitfires*, take the fighters."

"You heard the man," Higgins told us. "Let's go!"

Without even thinking, I rolled my *Spitfire* over, peeled off, and dove for the formation of German fighter planes just behind the guy in front of me.

This was, so far, my biggest engagement, and boy, was it a furball—airplanes everywhere, airplanes turning, diving, firing, some running for their lives, others chasing after the ones running. I did my best to remember everything we were taught in Operational Training—don't fly in a straight line, don't stay on a bandit's six for longer than five seconds, and *always look around*.

I was about to get on someone's six when I suddenly noticed someone was on *my* six. That someone being a German fighter. Automatically, I rolled my fighter on its side and turned. A moment later, the *Messerschmitt* roared past, and I got on his tail and waxed him.

This time, I saw the pilot bail out, and I watched the chute open. For some reason, I was grateful for that. At least I hadn't killed someone today. He was probably going to be a guest in a POW camp, but he'd had the poor taste to be an enemy combatant.

A moment later, the *Low Fuel* light winked on. I announced, "Bingo Fuel!"

"That's it, lads," Higgins told us. "Let's head for home."

As it usually was, our squadron had been shuffled around some. Something didn't look right, but I couldn't tell what it was. What I did know was that Higgins sounded odd.

I found out what had happened after we returned to Exeter.

Once we got back to base, I climbed out of my *Spitfire* and noticed that some of the guys looked stunned, including Higgins.

"What's wrong?" I asked him.

"I think we lost someone," he told me.

"Who?"

"Your tent-mate, Holliday," he said quietly. "I saw him go down. I didn't see a chute. I was too busy trying not to get shot down myself."

"Don't blame yourself," I said. "Maybe it's time for a drink, if you know what I mean."

Higgins cracked a muted grin. "Indeed it is," he said. "But first, debriefing. Come on, lads."

"Yes, sir," I said.

Shit. That explained the premonition I'd been having all day — that feeling of dread. But I made myself put away my feelings and headed over to Dispersal for the debriefing.

Our squadron area was quite subdued for a while after debriefing.

I'd added a third confirmed kill to my tally, a fighter this time. That meant that I'd now have three swastikas on my *Spitfire*. Two more kills and I'll be an ace, a fact of which I'm proud, until I remembered that each plane I've shot down meant that at least one man wasn't going to be returning to base or to his family, although this one at least was able to bail out. The most stunning news of all was when the Group Captain came over himself to tell me congratulations—for my promotion to Flying Officer or First Lieutenant.

I stood there, unable to say a thing as all the guys offered their congratulations.

But we got the best news of all just as we were about to knock off for the day. Twilight was settling down over the land when a Royal Army truck pulled up to the front gate, and someone got off. That someone turned out to be Holliday himself, or so we'd discovered once the guards had let him in, carrying his parachute with him.

"I just barely managed to bail out," he told us later, sipping from Higgins' flask. "I managed to pull my chute just in time and come down in the middle of an empty field somewhere in the middle of nowhere. I started walking pretty much anywhere when a Royal Army truck came along. I told him who I was and where I was based at. He told me Exeter was five klicks away and gave me a ride. And here I am."

We cheered, toasting him, the rest of the base joining us.

That night, our tent was loud and boisterous. It took a long while for us to get to sleep. Holliday's bubbly tasted even better that night.

CHAPTER SEVEN

Tuesday, 20 August 1940

The last week has been crazy. Brutal, one might say. And the pace isn't letting up, although we did get a short break, thanks to bad weather over the Channel for a few days. Since then, they've sent not one but three raids to bomb Middle Wallop, which dealt it a blow but never took it out of action for very long. The very next day, it was back in service after one raid. That was yesterday.

I'm waiting for the day when they hit Exeter. It's only a matter of time. I just hope we can brush it off just as easily.

In the meantime, there's been word that Churchill is doing some kind of speech for the House of Commons today. Hopefully, we won't be busy when he makes the speech.

For once, the day was perfectly timed. We didn't scramble until half-past ten, with the sun already high in the sky, the morning mist long since burned off. I didn't get any confirmed kills this time, but I still counted the mission as a success because I came back to base in one piece.

The afternoon was turning into a hazy evening when Higgins said, "You lot! Listen to this!" And he turned up the volume on the radio while we crowded around to listen.

"Today's lead story concerns the Prime Minister, who made a speech in the House of Commons. I'm afraid we don't have any recordings, but we did manage to get the text of the speech, and I will read a few excerpts of it for you . . ."

I'm afraid I tuned out much of the speech, until —

"The gratitude of every home in our Island, in our Empire, and indeed throughout the world, except in the abodes of the guilty, goes out to the British airmen who, undaunted by odds, unwearied in their constant challenge and mortal danger, are turning the tide of the world war by their prowess and by their devotion. Never in the field of human conflict was so much owed by so many to so few."

We were too drained at the moment to care, but from then on, we—the fighter pilots of the Royal Air Force—would be forever known from then on as *The Few*.

The next several days did not let up. The Luftwaffe paid us a visit every day, even Ten Group.

Then one day, the worst happened—a raid was headed straight for Exeter. On that day, I bagged a twin-engined *Bf-110*, although the rear gunner almost bagged me, but when we got back to base, we were horrified to discover *bomb craters*—scattered all over the base.

None of them, however, had come close to the runway. That, at least, was operational. Unfortunately, we'd also suffered losses, both in the air and on the ground.

Nobody in our squadron had bought it, but one pilot in each of the three other squadrons had, as well as about five people on the ground. That number was being refined by medics, also known as bodysnatchers, the poor people whose responsibility it was to check the wounded, people held in more respect than possibly us fighter pilots.

As the wounded were taken to the hospital, an earth-moving crew came in to smooth over the bomb craters. Within a few days, they would be gone, as if they'd never been there at all. The recovering wounded, depending on their wounds, would return to duty within days or weeks. Those who didn't, would eventually be replaced.

In short, we would be back in action the next day, a little

shaken, down but not out.

I was almost weak with relief when I found out Devon hadn't been counted among the dead or wounded, although she had a smudged cheek that bore mute testimony of her experience.

That fourth confirmed kill was the last one I claimed credit for during the Battle of Britain. That was the first week of September, as I recall.

The next week everything changed.

Monday, 16 September 1940

The Germans have made a big mistake.

And it all started with one of their planes getting lost and bombing London by mistake instead of its assigned target. Whatever its intended target was, we'll never know. What we do know was that in reprisal, Bomber Command sent its aircraft to Berlin. Hitler went nuts and ordered the Luftwaffe to turn its attention to British cities instead of RAF airfields — a move which gave us overwhelmed fighter pilots something we desperately needed, which was rest and a chance to replace our lost planes and pilots and to get our breath back and on our feet once again.

I'm not sure if the Luftwaffe knew what a desperate state we were in, but Hitler's decision, made in the heat of anger, was what decided the course of the battle, although that took a few days.

Here in Ten Group, things have dialed back quite a bit.

The next day was just like the day before had been — the phone in Dispersal hadn't rang once all day, although I did get sent out on patrols almost every day with a different wingman each time, which was better than sitting here waiting, at least while I was in the air.

We did, however, get a surprise visitor during the week.

A few of us were lounging about, talking about nothing in particular, when a strange officer came into Dispersal one day and spoke with Higgins for a few minutes.

"Edwards! Cooper! You lot come over here!"

Exchanging a confused look with Chris, we both rose from our chairs and went to Dispersal, chuckles following us.

"You rang, sir?" I asked for the both of us.

"Yes," Higgins said. "This is Wing Commander Richard Owens. He has a little proposal for you. I'll let him explain."

"Thank you, Higgins," the new officer said. He, like Higgins, was almost exactly the same height, but unlike Higgins, he was much more reserved, almost stern. He was clean-shaven, his sandy brown hair neatly trimmed and close-cropped, wearing an RAF sweater over a shirt and tie, as I'd seen some other officers do, and three stripes on his shoulder. "How would you gentlemen like to be on the first all-American fighter squadron?"

Chris and I exchanged delighted looks.

"Are you serious, sir?" I asked for the both of us.

"Absolutely," he said with a crisp nod. Looking at me, he said, "I understand from Higgins that you have *four* confirmed kills to your credit. Is that correct?"

"Yes, sir," I said.

"Impressive," he told me.

"Thank you, sir," I said as humbly as possible.

"We're going to have work on that," he said. "Get you that fifth kill."

"Beg your pardon, sir?"

"I could use someone with a record like that," he said.

"For what, sir?" I asked.

Then he gave us the details. A squadron of American pilots was being put together, to be called an Eagle Squadron, a reference to the eagle symbol on American passports. At some later date, more eagle squadrons might be formed, depending on how many more Americans arrived, but for the moment, just one squadron was to be formed, with a native RAF squadron leader and RAF flight leaders, at first, which could also change as time went on. This came from the highest levels of government, as he explained to us.

Following the successful Battle of Britain, as it was being called, other squadrons were being put together featuring pilots from other nations, so we Americans were hardly alone in this. It was just as much a smart military strategy as public relations to take pilots from various nations and put them in their own squadrons, or so he said.

"Did Churchill come up with this?" I asked.

"I'm afraid I don't know," Owens replied. "But regardless, I'm here to offer you the chance to sign up for the very first Eagle Squadron. You chaps are agreeable, then?" Owens asked.

"Yes, sir," we both said.

"Well then, I shall have the transfer orders made up. I expect we'll be seeing each other again very soon. Carry on, then."

"Thank you, sir," we chorused, both of us saluting him as one man.

Owens exchanged salutes with us, then swiftly departed without fanfare.

Behind us, Higgins said, "Well, it appears you chaps will be leaving us soon. I'll be sad to see you both go."

We turned around to face him.

"Thank you, sir," I said for the both of us. "It was an honor to fly with you."

"No, the honor was all mine," he said, rising from his desk to address us directly. "And mind you, it's not over yet."

"No, sir," I replied, agreeing because he was right.

Over the next several days, the Luftwaffe sortied just about every fighter plane and bomber they had that was based in the north of France, and in response, the RAF sent out just about every fighter plane Eleven and Twelve Group had. Meanwhile, we here in Ten Group in the southwest sector of England sat twiddling our thumbs, but I didn't make the decisions. Meanwhile, losses on both sides were heavy — and it broke the back of the Luftwaffe.

At the end of September, we received the best news we'd gotten all year — Operation Sea Lion, the planned invasion of the British Isles, had been postponed until further notice. It was notable as the first major defeat Nazi Germany had suffered so far, after an unbroken string of victories all across Western Europe.

We were elated — not just us, the whole squadron, the whole base, the whole Royal Air Force. And for Chris and I, there was a transfer to get ready for. Although, that wouldn't happen for another few weeks. But we couldn't celebrate just yet. As the saying went, there was a war on.

CHAPTER EIGHT

Wednesday, 1 October 1941

The Battle of Britain is a distant memory. But there's still work to do.

There's both good news and bad news. The good news is that, now that there's no longer the threat of daily air attack or imminent invasion, the Royal Air Force is now free to take the fight to the Luftwaffe. The bad news is that we now have the same problems Luftwaffe pilots had while flying in British airspace – if we get shot down, that means bailing out over enemy territory and the possibility of spending the rest of the war as a POW.

However, more good news, the best of which is that the first Eagle Squadron was so successful that a second squadron has been formed, and guess who got a second promotion, to Leftenant. Yes, that would be me. The only bad news is that Chris and I have been separated. He's still in the first squadron.

Right at the moment, our new squadron has been doing training workups in preparation for flying convoy escort, providing friendly air cover for convoys, which there have been quite a few. That means that yours truly doesn't stand a chance of getting shot down over Occupied France. Sadly, it also means I don't stand a chance of making ace, either.

More later.

As was the custom, we arose with the rising of the sun.

With morning mist still hanging on the trees in spiderweb tendrils, we shuffled off to get breakfast. Then, once we had good strong British coffee in us, we went to attend the pre-flight briefing.

We were going to rendezvous with a huge 80-ship convoy that was somewhere in the North Sea. The convoy was spotted by a recon aircraft yesterday, but contact was lost when the ships passed through a storm at sea.

We were told in no uncertain terms that it was essential that we discover at once where the convoy was and where it was headed. Once in the North Sea, they would have been well within the range of Luftwaffe aircraft based in Norway and Belgium.

Therefore, time was critical. That also meant our squadron was done doing training workups, and they were finally setting us loose.

In fact, just last summer, we'd had a ceremony of sorts, indicating we were ready to begin training maneuvers—and earning a visit from King George himself. I was absolutely quaking in my uniform, but the King was a good guy, wearing an RAF uniform. He came to review the squadron, which he was doing without comment until he stopped on a dime.

"And what do we have here?"

"Leftenant Matthew Cooper, Your Majesty," I said.

"Am I to understand that you have four confirmed kills from the Battle of Britain?"

"Yes, Your Majesty," I said.

"Hopefully, I can return to decorate you when you get that fifth kill," he said with a twinkle in his eye. "Until then, bide your time, and don't be a hero."

"Yes, Your Majesty," I said.

The rest of the inspection passed by in a blur.

Our *Spitfires* had been readied for flight, so all we had to do was suit up and head out to the flight line, where our aircraft were waiting, sitting on the runway. Unlike the improvised runway made of pierced steel planks in Exeter, here at North Weald, about an hour west of London, we had a real paved runway—much nicer, in my opinion.

In full flying kit, I jogged out to my aircraft—a *Spitfire* with dark gray and dark green stripes above and light gray underneath, with the letters *L OV* on the fuselage, painted in huge black letters, which caused me no end of chuckles—climbed on the left wing and eased down, holding on to the windshield frame.

The next minute or so was busy. As I tested the control surfaces, my crew chief helped me strap on the airplane. As I did so, I noticed one of the new kids climb into his *Spitfire* next to mine, by the name of Eric Ibsen. The kid had just turned twenty-one, making him old enough to fly in the Eagle Squadrons. In my humble opinion, I thought he could've done with a bit further seasoning, but as I've said before, I didn't get to make the big decisions.

Something about the look on his face as he glanced my way gave me pause, but *just as we were about to take off* was not the time or the place to be bringing up sudden reservations to the squadron leader, who happened to also be American.

So I kept my mouth shut while the crew chief closed the side door, slid the canopy closed, and finally stepped clear of the aircraft as the wheel chocks were removed.

Ten minutes later, we were out over the North Sea, which was looking none too placid on this October day. I felt sympathy for any ships currently transiting this body of water on the way to the English Channel. Their crews would be having a tough time.

Much to my relief, we spotted the convoy not too far from its expected position. Thanks to broken cloud cover, it was difficult to get an accurate count, but between all the pilots in our squadron we managed to ascertain that the whole convoy was there.

In the middle of congratulating ourselves, a message came through over our radio earphones.

"Control to OVEN. We have enemy aircraft inbound to your location," a female voice reported.

"How many?"

"Looks like two squadrons. They're headed directly towards you. Over."

"Roger," our squadron leader replied. After a moment, he said, "All right, you guys. Get ready. We got bandits on the way. Keep your eyes open."

I turned my gaze from my instrument panel to the endless blue sky outside the canopy as I ordered my flight to start flying racetrack patterns, keeping the throttle low. I was thinking the radar people were wrong when we flew out of a bank of clouds—and there they were.

Just as the controller had said, there was a squadron's worth of twin-engine bombers, the wings heavy with bombs.

"Tally-ho," I said right away. "Bandits, my position and closing, four o'clock low!"

"You heard him, boys, let's go get'em."

The rest of the squadron joined us just as we were diving to attack, and soon, a real furball was shaping up.

Keeping an eye glued to the *Low Fuel* indicator on my instrument panel, I rolled my *Spitfire* over and dove for the nearest bomber, but a split-second later, my sights were filled with another *Spitfire* from our squadron.

I pulled out and rolled over just in time, getting out of the way.

But another second later, things got a lot more complicated. The escorts arrived. Only these weren't *Messerschmitts*, these were *Focke-Wulfs*. They were excellent fighter planes that we'd been hearing rumblings about from RAF Intelligence.

Unlike the *Messerschmitt*, the *Focke-Wulf* was powered by a radial engine. That gave it a real edge.

If it was a rat race before, it soon became a fight for survival.

Soon the little bastard that had cut me off had a bigger problem — a bandit was hot on his tail and getting ready to fire any second. But I got on his tail faster, got him in my sights, and fired.

The German had made a classic mistake. He was concentrating too hard on getting a confirmed kill. But now it was his plane that was plunging into the unforgiving North Sea.

"Good job, Cooper," the squadron leader said. "Ibsen, talk to me. You there?"

"Yes, sir," replied a decidedly shaky voice.

I wanted to chew his ass out right then and there. But right at that moment, my *Low Fuel* light winked on, so I called out, "Bingo fuel."

Our squadron formed up to return to base, by which time another squadron was arriving to take over for us. Once we were all safe and none of us had been lost, I couldn't decide whether I was happy Ibsen had survived or if I was going to kill him myself for cutting me off.

But I could worry about that later. If that kill was confirmed, I was now an Ace.

A few hours later, once all the after-action reports had been compiled, typed up, and taken to the brass, I now had *five* confirmed kills to my credit.

That meant that I would get a second Distinguished Flying Cross.

But celebrating would have to wait. Once the Squadron Leader, Jeff Blake, returned from a meeting with the brass, he found me and said, "Cooper, come with me for a minute."

"Yes, sir."

I followed him obediently over to Dispersal. On the way over, we found Ibsen, shooting the breeze with the other new pilots. Blake said, "Ibsen."

The boy snapped to attention. "Sir!"

"Come with us."

Ibsen went pale and gulped. "Yes, sir."

The three of us went over to Dispersal, me trying mightily to hold my tongue. Once there, Blake took his seat behind his desk and said, "Ibsen."

"Yes, sir?"

"Please give me one good reason why I shouldn't have your wings for the stunt you pulled."

"Sir—"

"You cut off Cooper here, and on top of that, you almost got yourself shot down!" He rose from his desk, red in the face, like I had been. "In short, you've done everything you shouldn't have done! You will not do these things again, or you will get sent back to training. Am I clear?"

The boy went even more pale and gulped. "Yes, sir."

"Anything you care to add, Leftenant Cooper? You're his flight leader."

"Yes, sir," I said, seeing my chance. I addressed Ibsen and said, "You pull some shit like that again, and I'll ground your ass myself. Do you copy?"

The boy's face went from merely pale to ashen. "Yes, sir."

"Good," Blake said coldly. "I believe that covers everything. Dismissed."

The boy pivoted smartly and marched away.

"You're going to make an excellent squadron leader someday, Cooper," he told me once Ibsen had left Dispersal.

"Thank you, sir," I replied.

"Go take some time," he told me next. "It's going to be a few hours until our aircraft are refueled and rearmed."

"Yes, sir," I said. "Thank you."

"And congratulations," he said next. "Not every day you become an ace."

I suddenly cracked a grin. "No, sir."

CHAPTER NINE

Friday, 5 December 1941

In the weeks since becoming an ace and getting the second DFC, our squadron hasn't seen a whole lot of action. I guess the Luftwaffe has decided that our supply convoys aren't worth the effort it takes to go after them – or they have bigger fish to fry elsewhere.

We learned that Hitler had decided to invade Soviet Russia back in September. We all shook our heads at that move. Since then, Britain has been getting a steady flow of Russian refugees.

Nazi Germany has made another big mistake. The word from the big brass is that Hitler had to be totally out of his fucking mind to take on Stalin.

Unfortunately, so far, Germany is doing well in Russia. Those same brass have Russia out of the war before too long.

Friday my squadron had our orders changed. From then on, we were no longer escorting convoys. Starting that day, we would instead be doing fighter sweeps, deliberately poking the bear to see what kind of a reaction we would get. The younger pilots were eager for this change in our mission. Many a convoy escort mission had ended with this entry in our logbooks – *No enemy activity encountered.*

But we also got shiny new *Spitfires*. These had new guns. Instead of all *Browning* machine guns, some of them had been replaced by a *Hispano* cannon in each wing.

Today's mission was going to be a big one, as I found out during the pre-flight briefing. We were actually going to be flying with Chris' squadron, due south over the Channel, and offer battle to the Luftwaffe.

Just over forty minutes later, we were back at base. I didn't claim any new confirmed kills, but I did get a probable added to my record. Plus, we didn't lose anyone, so on the whole, I counted our first fighter sweep as a successful mission.

But just as we were completing our after-action reports, an officer arrived in a vehicle, driving a little too fast. Soon after his arrival, I heard him ask, "You have a Leftenant Cooper here?"

"Yes, sir. Right over there."

"Thank you."

A moment later, I found myself gazing at an officer with bleach-blond hair and pale skin. "Leftenant Cooper?"

I saluted him because he had three stripes on his arm. "Yes, sir. What can I do for you?"

"Your wingman from three-oh-one squadron, Christopher Edwards. I'm afraid he's been killed in action today."

I felt hands on my shoulders. "Sorry, Cooper," someone said.

Meanwhile, I was floored. "How did he —"

"According to the after-action report, a bandit managed to get on his six and put a few rounds into his aircraft. Nobody knows how he managed to get back to base because when they pulled him out, he was badly wounded. They took him to the hospital, but he died on the operating table."

I literally had no words. The other officer rested his hand on my shoulder for a moment, then departed.

A few minutes later, Blake came to me and handed me a slip of paper.

"What's this?"

"A forty-eight-hour pass," he explained. "Get out of here. Go into town for two nights and a day. Don't let me see you until Sunday morning. Copy that, Cooper?"

"Yes, sir," I said. "Thank you, sir."

He clapped me on the shoulder. "Go blow off some steam. Get your head on straight."

"Yes, sir."

Somehow, war hits the hardest when it hits close to home when someone you know is killed in action.

Over the next few days, the people of North Weald would arrange a funeral for him, burying him next to their Catholic church. The RAF would collect his last effects, box them up, and send them home. I would drop a note in with the items.

I dearly hoped his family wouldn't posthumously disown him, but instead would be proud of their son for making the ultimate sacrifice because he died a hero. Hopefully, once the war was over, they would go to visit his grave.

But right at that moment, I got a vehicle from the motor pool and drove off the base straight to London, hoping to lose my grief in a mug of beer.

I'd left the base in the afternoon, reaching London in the early evening, just after sunset. Once in the city center, I found a suitably appropriate pub and made my way inside.

I had to stop to let an old man and his wife in first, but the old man said, "No, lad, you go in first. Royal Air Force always goes first."

"Oh, no, sir, please, go on ahead," I said.

The old man and his wife beamed at each other, then at me. "An officer and a gentleman," he said, tipping his hat to me. "Good evening, lad."

"Thank you, sir," I said, holding the door open for them.

Once they were inside, I quickly followed.

As I sat at the bar, I noticed there were several other uni-

forms present, who all either gave single nods of acknowledg-
ment of my presence or lifted their beer mugs.

A moment later, the bartender came over. "What can I get
for one of The Few?"

"I'll have a beer, thanks," I said.

"Coming right up, Leftenant."

A moment later, he set it down in front of me. I passed him
a five-pound note and began to sip at it, turning my stool to
observe the pub.

The place was larger than it looked from the outside, but at
the moment, there were more empty tables than occupied.

"Is this seat taken?"

I spun my chair around, searching for the source of that
female voice, to see a woman standing close by—slender,
platinum-blonde, fair, almost pale, wearing a white silk dress
buttoned up the front, and a hat on her head.

"Chair's open if you want," I said. "No need to stand on
my account."

After a moment, the lady took the stool next to mine, sat,
and crossed her legs. "It's not very often I see a Royal Air
Force pilot sitting by himself," she said.

"Sorry, but I wouldn't make very good company tonight."

"And why would you say such a thing?"

"A buddy of mine was killed in action today," I said sadly.

"Oh," she said. "I'm very sorry. Do you want to talk about
it?"

"Are you sure?" I asked. "If I start, I might not stop."

She smiled. "It's better to talk than not to," she said. "I'm
Clarice Ashmore."

"Leftenant Matt Cooper," I said, reaching out to shake
hands.

"Lovely to meet you, Matt," she said.

By dinner time, she got us a room in a nearby hotel so we

could, uhm, talk, in private. And talk, we did, once dinner had been carted away. In fact, we talked through the evening and all-day Saturday. That night, I went to bed feeling like I had a handle on the grief, if nothing else.

Alcohol and sex with a stranger could be very therapeutic that way.

The forty-eight hours away from the base did me a lot of good because the next day — everything changed.

Sunday, 7 December 1941

This was the day everything changed – the whole war – and how it affected both the Allies and the Axis powers.

We here in England didn't hear about the attack until about dinner time, and the mood in England was like a prayer had been granted, for the entire United Kingdom had been collectively wishing for the United States to get involved in the war.

The move by the Japanese to attack the US Pacific Fleet based at Pearl Harbor was roundly seen as the worst mistake they could have made, second only to Hitler's decision to attack Soviet Russia.

Analysts agreed it was now a whole new world war.

My arrival the next morning was met with welcome, followed by expressions of sympathy. Then we got to work with yet another fighter sweep over the English Channel. It was surprisingly easy to concentrate on my work.

It wasn't until sunset, and we were able to knock off for the day, that the squadron leader beckoned us over to the radio to listen.

"Hey, you guys! Listen to this!"

We came over to Dispersal to listen, and boy, did we hear a lot.

I was, without doubt, stunned to hear that the Japanese had attacked the Pacific Fleet based at Pearl Harbor, along with all the aircraft at Hickam. Dozens of aircraft had been destroyed on the ground, a dozen major warships had been damaged or outright sunk, and hundreds, if not thousands, of men had been killed or wounded in exchange for about a dozen Japanese planes.

It was a disaster of epic proportions for the United States, but the fallout from that disaster would take a few months to fully realize.

In the meantime, the mood here in England was of celebration.

That same week, I was called into the office of Group Captain Farmer. Not sure what this was about, I knocked on his door at the appointed time.

"Come in."

"Leftenant Matt Cooper, reporting as ordered, sir," I said, snapping to attention.

Farmer turned away from the window. "Cooper, there are you are. Come on in, have a seat."

I did as he said while he sat behind his desk.

"So, Cooper. I wanted to meet with you privately now that things have changed to let you know we're going to miss you."

"I'm sorry, miss me?"

"Cooper, you and your fellow Americans are going to be leaving us now that the US has officially joined the war."

"Yes, but that's not going to happen for months," I said. "At the least."

"How do you reckon?"

"Well, sir, it's going to take months to get on a war footing," I explained. "You have to understand, Americans have been isolationist for the last twenty years. It's going to take months for the military industrial complex to get off the ground."

"Months, you say?"

"At least," I said.

"Well, I'm chuffed to hear that," he said, suddenly brighter. "Because we wanted to make you Squadron Leader."

"I'm sorry, sir?"

"Yes," he said, smiling at my response. "Blake is going to be rotating out soon, and who better to replace him than you. What do you say?"

"I'd be honored," I said, and it was the truth.

"Jolly good," he said heartily, hitting his desk with his hand. "Well, Cooper, don't let me keep you. But don't tell anyone what we talked about. I want it to be a surprise when the time comes."

"Yes, sir," I said. "Not a word."

"Very good," he said. "Off with you, lad. Dismissed."

"Yes, sir."

I left his office in disbelief. *Squadron Leader!* It was too bad I had nobody to tell. I couldn't even write home about it.

CHAPTER TEN

Tuesday, 1 September 1942

Today was a grim anniversary – the beginning of the darkest
years of our lives so far.

But for us American RAF pilots, it represents a whole new beginning. Personnel from the US Army Air Force, as it was now
known, have begun to arrive in the area over the summer.

Negotiations will now begin in earnest, if they haven't already,
with the Royal Air Force to transfer the Eagle Squadrons to the
Eighth Air Force, just beginning to set up shop.

I'm sure I'll have more to add later.

Over the summer, advanced elements of what was now
known as the Eighth Air Force had arrived in England and
had set-up shop. Shortly after that, they'd begun to negotiate
with the Royal Air Force to begin the process of transferring
the Eagle Squadrons to US control.

But that wasn't all that had happened. In June, the US Navy
scored a huge victory at the Battle of Midway. The Japanese
had tried to lure elements of the Pacific Fleet into battle, hoping to destroy them, leaving the way clear to Hawaii and,
eventually, the West Coast.

Instead, codebreakers had been able to divine Japanese in-
tentions, and the Pacific Fleet had been lying in wait. The Japanese lost four fleet aircraft carriers at Midway, a shocking
defeat after an unbroken string of victories across the South
Pacific.

Here in England, however, things were just starting to get off the ground, if you'll pardon the phrase. The Eighth Air Force people had been negotiating all summer long with the Royal Air Force, and now us Eagle pilots were reporting to a processing center to see to the details.

Today was my turn.

I confidently marched into the processing center and snapped to attention. My stomach churned when I saw who one of the officers were at the table—none other than Nathan Nate Hughes, now wearing the silver oak leaves of a Lieutenant Colonel.

"Squadron Leader Matthew Cooper, reporting as ordered, *sir*!"

The ranking officer, a general, smiled as he said, "At ease, sir, please."

I adopted a more casual pose, putting my arms behind my back.

"This board has been established for the transfer of personnel from the Royal Air Force to the US Army Air Forces. You're ready to join?"

"Yes, sir," I said.

"Very well," the general said. "Colonel Hughes?"

Meanwhile, Hughes looked up from my file, open in front of him, and said, "Squadron Leader. Certified ace with five confirmed kills. Impressive."

Despite myself, I smiled. "Thank you, sir."

"Unfortunately, we can't give you the rank of Major. We're only planning three squadrons, and since you're the leader of the fourth squadron, I'm afraid the best we can do is to give you the rank of Captain. You would be a flight leader."

Apparently, they must have seen the look on my face.

"Squadron Leader Cooper, if it helps you feel better, the next time a squadron leader rotates out, we will give you the slot. That's the best we can do."

I bit back my rejoinder that might have gotten me court-martialed and instead said, "Yes, sir. I understand."

"Very good," the general said. "We'll now have you take the oath and have you sworn in."

"Yes, sir," I said.

Once all was said and done, I walked out into bright sunshine, feeling thoroughly betrayed and done dirty, as though they'd taken all my service and flushed it down the toilet.

Somehow, I didn't start cursing, even though I wanted to.

But it wasn't all bad news — the pay would be much better, as would the food. No offense to the Royal Air Force, but their idea of food left much to be desired.

Just as I was pondering the unfairness of it all, a female voice called to me. "Matt? Is that you?"

Having heard my name, I naturally turned to see *Cathy*!

Without missing a beat, she ran into my arms and threw herself against me, staying like that for a minute.

When she pulled back, I saw she was wearing US Army green, two stripes on each shoulder. "Oh my god, Matthew! I knew it was you!"

"Hi, Cathy," I said, accepting a kiss on the cheek.

"Oh my god, dear, I can't believe it's you," she said breathlessly, pulling back. "I see you managed to get on the Royal Air Force."

"Look at you," I said. "I see you joined up, too."

"Well, they took all the *Clipper* planes and commandeered them for government service," she said dryly. "So I kind of had to come with it."

"Boy, they're not messing around," I said.

"No, sir," she agreed. "Let's have dinner."

Before I could enthusiastically agree, a male voice behind me said, "Captain?"

Turning away from Cathy, I faced a pilot from my now former squadron. "Yes?"

"Hate to interrupt, but duty calls. We gotta get back to the base, sir."

"Yes, we do," I said. "Get the men together."

"Yes, sir," he said.

I turned back to face Cathy. "I heard," she said. "It's all right. Go do what needs to be done, and I'll see you later. Okay?"

"Right," I said. "You know where to find me?"

"I know where to find you," she assured me softly. "Later, dear."

Tuesday, 29 September 1942

It's official. Today we were officially handed over from the Royal Air Force to the US Eighth Air Force. We're now the Fourth Fighter Group, having the honor of being the first such unit in England. It remained to be seen what sort of missions we would draw, but for today, we were just settling in once all the pomp and circumstance was done.

I haven't decided yet what I'm going to do with my RAF dog tags. I might keep them.

This is going to be my last diary entry. Who knows — maybe someone will read this.

EPILOGUE

I put the note from my grandfather back inside the diary and closed the cover, putting one of the rubber bands back on.

I couldn't decide whether or not I wanted to read it again. Granted, I was proud of my grandfather in a way that words couldn't express, but pride was tempered with disbelief. I hadn't had so much as an inkling of what he'd done.

"Are you okay?" Annie sat next to me on the hotel couch as I'd read the diary.

"It's going to take a while for me to process all this," I said as I put the diary back in the box.

"I know," she said, rubbing my back. "But just remember Grand-dad Matt was a good man who taught you how to fly."

I chuckled. "Right. Thanks." I gave her a kiss full of love.

"Want to go downstairs and have dinner?"

"Sounds good. I need to get out of here before we have to go back home."

"I understand," Annie said. "If you need to talk, remember, I'm here."

"I know," I told her. "I love you."

She smiled. "I love you, too. Now let's go have dinner."

The End

ABOUT THE AUTHOR

Jon Bradbury is celebrating 20 years as a published author with eXtasy Books, beginning with *Colorblind* in 2004. Some of his other titles include *The Football Player's Wife, Midnight Blue, We'll Always Have Paris,* and *Sugar Daddy.*